MW01248990

Pleading Eyes
for Lorelei

By: Vicki Boartfield

∞INFINITY
PUBLISHING

Copyright © 2014 by Vicki Boartfield

ISBN 978-0-7414-7156-7

Printed in the United States of America

This is a work of fiction. Names, characters, places, and incidents either are the product of the author's imagination or are used fictitiously. Any resemblance to actual events or locales or persons, living or dead, is entirely coincidental. Certain names of individuals have been changed for the purpose of this novel. Other names used with permission.

Published February 2014

INFINITY PUBLISHING
1094 New DeHaven Street, Suite 100
West Conshohocken, PA 19428-2713
Toll-free (877) BUY BOOK
Local Phone (610) 941-9999
Fax (610) 941-9959
Info@buybooksontheweb.com
www.buybooksontheweb.com

Thank You:

Thanks to all who assisted in editing, research and review of the materials for this novel. A special thank you to my caring husband who inspired me to fulfill my lifelong dream.

In Loving Memory,
Dr. Lorelei Yvonne Flora Guidry Eckey
July 8, 1929 – April 18, 1986

TABLE OF CONTENTS

Introduction:

"Men are said to succumb to her spell, just by casting a glance her way. But Lorelei is more than an enchanted mermaid: she's a legendary beauty, tourist magnet and employer. The quiet Rhine village of Assmannshausen is home to about 1,000 residents. Here, the boardwalk is mostly comprised of jetties reaching out into the river. A woman with sunglasses and a loud voice is perched on one of the piers, pitching boat rides to passersby. "A trip to Lorelei for you?" she calls to strolling tourists. Across from her, a handful of people have gathered. They sit on benches and watch as a ship approaches the landing. The tourist ship travels down the Rhine to Lorelei - or more accurately the rock named after her. Armed with cool drinks and ice cream, the visitors settle into their seats on the sunny top deck of the boat. They hail from around the globe."

http://www.dw.de/under-the-spell-of-the-lorelei/a-16998872

Chapter One:

Round-the-World Trip

On a warm sunny day in the Summer of 1964, Lorelei sat slenderly dressed in her favorite turquoise swimsuit in the tourist boat looking at her legendary reflection, thinking happy thoughts. She tossed her fine, curly brown hair from her eyes towards the gentle breeze and smiled. She felt herself as beautiful as "The Lorelei," with her tan complexion, luring figure and starry eyes. She always wondered why she was named after "The Lorelei." She had several crushes in high school, but in her senior year, had fallen in love with Fred from her Church, who was five years older. She had lovingly lured him to the altar fifteen years ago, 1949, in Adrian, Michigan.

She had romantic thoughts of her husband home in Boston: his dark brown wavy hair, his prominent aristocratic nose, his big wonderful smile and slim body that matched her own. She missed him terribly. This was not the first time Lorelei had left him for a tour of Europe. Two years before in 1962, she had travelled and studied languages with her Aunt Hope, a Language Professor from Adrian College who never married. She sang at Lorelei's wedding, the beautiful hymn, "Love" by Mary Baker Eddy. They had toured France, Spain, Switzerland, Italy, Monaco, Austria, Germany, Denmark, Holland, Belgium, Sweden, Amsterdam, England and Scotland.

This time Lorelei was in her final day of the "110-Day" *Round-the-World* trip with the "Seven Seas Educational Tour Group." The ship was called *The Seven Seas*, with an all German-speaking crew and chartered by the University of the Seven Seas. It was a medium-sized ship with six decks and a bridge with about 250 students, 25 faculty members, 250 crew, 25 staff and 27 who were called "Adult World Seminar" people. Lorelei was one of the seminar people. Most of them were retired, and Lorelei was the youngest among them. They spent almost four months on the ship!

The students had classes six days a week at sea, and the adult seminar members could attend any classes they wanted, but were not suppose to participate, as the classes were not for credit. Lorelei participated in the *Theatre History Course* and in a *German* class towards the end of the trip and went to *Area Studies* for two hours each morning. It was a good course that helped her prepare for the ports they were to visit: Portugal, Spain, Italy, Greece, Lebanon, Egypt, India, Ceylon, Malaysia, Thailand, the Philippines, Hong Kong, Taiwan and Japan. They were also scheduled to spend a one-day holiday in Hawaii. They stayed five days in Japan, but only two days in all other ports.

Lorelei discovered to her surprise that she enjoyed the Asian countries the most, particularly Thailand, Taiwan, Japan and Hong Kong. She learned the economics of travel, in a short span of time. She felt she ought to be able to hire herself out as a future travel guide and could show anyone how to travel without having to rely on American Express!

She had a wonderful, productive Summer and was able to speak Italian, German and French fluently. On her return to the States, she knew she would be in the backdrop of the U.S. Civil Rights Act, of legislation that prohibited discrimination and ended racial segregation in the schools. She would be student teaching and working as a novice writer. She would also be entering into her graduate studies, writing about the effects of the Civil Rights Act within the theatre environment. But now it was time to get back to her passionate husband, Fred. She wanted to talk to him about starting a family. Several years ago, when she thought she was pregnant, he told her how relieved he was that she was not.

He explained to her at that time that he really did not want any children, because their children would be the Church. He was a devoted writer for the Church, and Lorelei was also actively involved as a soloist and reader. However, she was ready to talk to him, to give him reasons why they should have a family to promote their faith to future generations. Lorelei respected and believed in her ancestors and wanted descendants. She had vowed to be the family researcher ever since the day that her mother had disappeared, when she was a teenager. She would not think of that tragic time for the moment. She would only concentrate on persuading her Fred to start a family of their own, when she returned!

Chapter Two:

The Unexpected

A week later, Lorelei hugged and kissed her husband at the General Edward Lawrence Logan International Airport in Boston. He was dressed in a handsome, black suit with a white tie and gave her a smile with his huge white teeth. She greeted him in white slacks and a black, ruffled low-cut blouse. Her wavy brown hair bounced in excitement, and her rosy cheeks were flushed. She had emotional tears in her eyes and looked into his. There was something missing in his eyes. She thought maybe it was their four-month absence from each other, or perhaps he was focused on his work as a writer for the Church Monitor. She knew he was currently writing a follow-up article about President John F. Kennedy's tragic assassination, and its effects on college students majoring in politics. So, they walked out of the airport, and Fred told her he wanted to take her to lunch at a new restaurant and hear all about her trip. Of course, they had written letters to each other during her European tour, and she had sent him dozens of post cards, but he said he wanted to hear every detail.

Fred chose a quiet corner table in the new German diner called, "The Jacob Wirth," and ordered Reuben stix and tea. Fred smiled nervously across from his wife, his Bostonian voice brittle, as he whispered her nickname: "Sweet." She smiled back, excited to tell him her details. The waitress took their order for pretzel salmon, and Lorelei dramatically began to recall her adventures. She told him about swimming and basking in the wonderful Mediterranean, of the tall mountain peaks, the primitive sculptures, the theatres and cathedrals. She shared stories about her observations in the libraries and museums. After almost 30 minutes without catching her breath, she concluded it would take a life-time to share the wonders she wanted to personally show him. In the faint background, they listened to the Beatles' song, "Yesterday." They discussed their music: "Beatlemania," and Fred told her how the Beatles had become distinguished, international British pop stars. They both loved their music.

After finishing their delicious salmon and beet salad, Fred reached over to hold Lorelei's hands. He sighed: "Sweet, I need to tell you something." He cleared his throat and continued: "You know I love you. You know that I would never want to hurt you." Lorelei stopped eating and stared into his eyes. He hesitated: "But, Lorelei, I met someone this Summer while you were away. She is actually from our Church, and you know and love her also! You remember Manette from our Church?" Lorelei carefully nodded. She remembered Manette, a young girl of twenty-five, with beautiful long, blond hair, petite and fragile, who worked as the secretary in the Monitor office. Thoughts raced through Lorelei's mind of how different she was from the timid and shy Manette. Fred continued, "Manette and I have been working together on a special project for the Monitor. She and I have eaten out a couple times, and we both realized that we had a lot in common. She loves to stay at home and cook, and her hobbies include interior decorating." He abruptly concluded: "She and I want to be married!" Lorelei just looked back at him, tears running down her cheeks, her beautiful sad lips quivered. She could not believe what she was hearing. She cried, "Fred, how could this have happened? Why did you not tell me in your letters?" Fred guiltily squeaked, "I could not possibly ruin your European tour!" Fred continued to hold Lorelei's hands in his own, but she suddenly moved his hands away, as if he had just given her some type of disease. She excused herself and told him that she could not sit there any longer. She told him to take her home, so they could make plans for divorce.

Chapter Three:

A New Beginning

Two months later, Lorelei was on her way down Interstate 90 from Boston, Massachusetts to Clinton, Iowa in her brand-new, blue 1970 Dodge Aries. Her father, Don, who lived in Michigan and was a lawyer, had processed the divorce settlement through the mail. Lorelei received the money from the sales of the exclusive, Boston waterfront property and sailboat that Fred had given to her as a wedding gift fifteen years ago. In turn, she agreed to leave Fred their three hundred thousand dollar home and all furnishings. It was not quite the compensation for a broken heart, but it gave Lorelei enough money to begin a new life for herself in a new city.

Lorelei had applied and been offered a drama teaching position at Clinton Community College. She felt she had no choice but to start over in a new town, where at least she knew some of her paternal ancestors had lived. She also decided to continue her doctorate program and would have plenty of time to research and write her thesis. She would not have time to think of Fred or her tender heart. At least, there were no children involved. She would purchase a mobile home in Clinton and be able to finance her Ph.D. studies. She could have gone to live close to her younger sister, Donna Marie, in Georgia, or to her father in Michigan, or with her other siblings, Donald, Marty or Elaine in Florida, but she knew they were busy trying to establish their careers, and she did not want to interfere. So, Lorelei took her shattered heart and replaced it with determination and faith that a new door would open for her. She was in her thirties and knew she was still attractive and appealing, but next time she would be careful about "luring a man to the altar."

In September, Lorelei began teaching drama to about sixty multi-racial students. Most were from the farms in Iowa. As Lorelei researched the Ph.D. programs, she discovered the true meaning of "friendly." Friendly was what she needed at that time, especially after investigating two other universities, finding one inhospitable to the fact that she was two years over the usual age they wanted to accept into their Ph.D. program, and the other one cold, cold, — not only in a cold climate, but impersonal and forbidding in their approach. So, almost incidentally, Lorelei found herself deciding to get her degree at the University of Iowa after the department head was so friendly. Lorelei decided to complete her doctorate degree in theatre, because she remembered a compliment from a former staff mentor, who told her she was a natural teacher for the dramatic arts.

By Fall Semester of 1969, Lorelei completed her dissertation of the Hôtel de Bourgogne and received her Ph.D. in Theatre Arts. The dissertation was her study of France's first public theatre of the pre-classical era, and its influence and development on French theatres and drama. She continued teaching at the Community College level. She taught part-time English, Speech and Theatre classes at Southeastern Community and Iowa Wesleyan Colleges. She applied at the University level, but found she was "too highly qualified." They told her they could not provide the appropriate salary. Even though Lorelei, as a single woman, was not involved or interested in the political arena of the gay rights movement that occurred that year, she wondered if sex discrimination was part of the reason they had rejected her. She felt that her rigorous eight years of study had been for naught, and it was a cruel reminder of her divorce.

Lorelei found a nice Church nearby in Iowa City of about one hundred members. She met a single woman her age, Celia, and they became good friends. They complemented each other with their differences. Lorelei was boisterous and high-strung, especially when she sang in Church, and Celia sang quiet and low. Lorelei was bold and dramatic, and Celia was simple and plain. Lorelei dressed in loud colors and bouncy, decorative hats, and Celia wore sack dresses and boots, as a farmer's daughter. Lorelei confided in Celia of her one flaw: "When I was a child about eight, my mother took me to the doctor against my father's wishes to clean out the wax in my left ear. The doctor's assistant was inexperienced, and she damaged my eardrum. I have been deaf in my left ear ever since. So, that is why I sing and talk louder to compensate for my deafness in one ear." Celia hugged Lorelei. In her soft voice, she reassured her: "I am so sorry you had to go through such an ordeal. Thank goodness you can hear out of your right ear. I know you must feel self-conscious at times, but please be reassured that your loveliness, inside and out, compensates for any flaw you think you may have. You are a beautiful woman, Lorelei, and I know that my father, Otto, and my Uncle Ted, have looked more than once at your radiance." Lorelei thanked her for the special compliments.

Lorelei went on several casual dates with men that Celia introduced to her. Celia did not date at all. Lorelei wished she could be more like Celia, but realized she wanted to love again. She preferred to date only men from the Church. However, she remembered from her European tours both in '62 and '64 that if she had not been married to Fred, at the time, she could have developed casual, romantic relationships with several foreign men she had encountered. She smiled as she thought of the gazes the men gave her when she sunbathed in her favorite, slender turquoise bathing suit on the beaches of the Mediterranean Sea.

She had not thought of the incident for a long time, but remembered one, very special Italian gentleman she had met at an Italian Comedy Theatre. She recalled wearing a similar gown to her former wedding dress, a white satin gown with a low-cut back, and a corsage of her favorite red and white carnations and chrysanthemums. Her long, dark brown hair was pulled up in a French twist with a beautiful French white comb. It was during *Intermission* that she walked in the lobby to get a drink of water. When she turned around, standing behind her was a handsome, tall, middle-aged Italian man with black, perfect, combed-back hair. She could not help but notice his smoky, dark suit, white, perfectly starched shirt and black satin tie. His resemblance to Sean Connery, the *James Bond* character in the movies, was uncanny. He smiled at her, and she heard his sexual voice whisper: "Sei bellissima!" Lorelei thanked him for his compliment, in Italian, as she knew the language well from her European tours.

Their eyes met for just one moment, as if time had stopped for them alone. In English, he spoke again: "Pardon me, Bella donna. Are you enjoying the comic clowns in the *Commedia dell'arte*?" Their faces turned towards each other, and she stood up straight and replied in her lovely Bostonian, Soprano voice: "Oh yes, I love the constant surprises and histrionic abilities of the medieval stages they represent." He took her arm slightly away from the water fountain, so that they could let others behind them drink. He wanted to continue their discussion. He probed gently: "What do you think of the character, Harlequin, who dearly loves Columbine, and of the mischievous clown who tries to separate them?" Lorelei replied, "Oh, yes, it is so comical and yet, so romantic, at the same time!" He continued, "You know this clown play was originally a slapstick adaptation of the *Commedia dell'arte*, which originated in my hometown in Italy in the 16th century!" "No, I did not know that!" exclaimed

Lorelei. She was excited talking with the Italian man, who also seemed to love the theatre as much as she did. Their arms accidentally touched as he described the clowns with gestures, and Lorelei felt a touch of immediate attraction between them. However, before they could exchange names, a blond-haired, middle-aged, tall debutante-type woman walked up to her Italian acquaintance, and said in a rather demanding Italian tone: "Honey, it is time to get back to the play. Intermission is over." He did not make introductions. He only bowed politely to Lorelei and in farewell said, "It was very nice to talk with you. Enjoy." She smiled back at him, and stood there in a trance, as she noticed that the debutante had on her left ring finger, a huge Italian-designed sapphire wedding ring. She said to herself, "Ah, me," and went back to her seat to enjoy the rest of the play.

Chapter Four:

Farmer Ted

Lorelei first encountered Ted at Church along with his wife, Cleo. Lorelei simply knew him as Celia's uncle, who, along with her father Otto, sometimes drove up to Iowa City to Church, which was an hour's trip away. At the time, the brothers looked very much alike to Lorelei, as she thought to herself: "faded, short, full of figure, somewhat tired, out-of-style, small brimmed felt hats, even in the Summer." Lorelei surmised that easily both of them could have been carved as Hummel figurines, with their quaint Germanic features, large bulbous noses, ruddy complexions and bulging, pleading brown eyes. They wore one-piece suits that bagged around the legs that always needed pressing and nondescript neckties.

Ted became a widower the next year. His wife, Cleo, had died at the young age of 59 from cancer. Church members whispered together about her lengthy illness, and how devoted he was by her deathbed. It was a great shock to him, and so his farm was greatly neglected. He had to come out of his misery, if he wanted to save his farm.

Several months later, Ted travelled to Iowa City and asked Lorelei out to lunch. Lorelei had decided not to judge a person by his age, or appearance, although she knew Ted was 22 years her senior. She felt it could not hurt, anyway, to go out with Celia's uncle, and Celia confided in her that he was a very kind and lonely man. Lorelei prided herself in being open-minded. She also felt it might be a good diversion from her student papers and lesson plans.

Ted took Lorelei to a country café in town. Lorelei, by that time, was in her late thirties, still very attractive and slender. On that day, she wore a turquoise cotton dress and matching broad-brimmed hat that slanted casually over one of her eyes. Ted wore his one-piece brown suit and white neck-tie. They sat out under the canopy. Music from Loretta Lynn, "Songs from My Heart," was streaming from the small speaker above. Ted was shy as he asked her what she would like to order. Lorelei ordered a chef salad, and Ted ordered ham and vegetables. As they sat enjoying their surroundings, Lorelei mused that Ted was indeed much her senior, though that was neither here nor there to her. Though, she thought to herself, that he was not the sort of person she would have picked out, looking around, for a future husband. It never would have occurred to her. Lorelei also noticed as they sat making small talk, how the grime had settled under the nails of his short, stocky, weather-worn fingers, that his square face had a perpetual five-o'clock shadow look, and his neck and hands were reddened with the outdoors. There could be no doubt he was a farmer, and Lorelei's father had always taught her to respect farmers. She thought about how her father had grown up as a farmer in Indiana, and his father before him in Iowa, and had taught Lorelei and her siblings how to raise gardens. There was something sacred and honorable about anyone who actually was a farmer, so Lorelei respected, rather than scorned, the signs of that trade on Ted.

As the dessert of strawberry shortcake was served, Ted, although awkward and earnest, launched into a conversation about how lonesome he had been since he lost Cleo. Lorelei assured him that it was not so bad to live alone; that she had lived alone and thoroughly enjoyed it. It was not until later that Lorelei learned from Celia, that Ted had decided he was interested in marrying her and purposely, had come up to Iowa City to court her. Celia also told her that he had been very disappointed when he had learned she was about to go on another tour of Europe with her nephew and two teenagers.

However, before her Summer European Tour, Lorelei and Ted had lunch after Church several times. Lorelei joked with the people in the faculty lounge about her farmer who was bringing her apples and melons. Yet, they were not from his farm. He bought them on Muscatine Island on the way to Iowa City. Lorelei had not realized how far away his farm was, and that he was travelling to Celia and Lorelei's Church every week, just to have lunch with her.

Lorelei wanted to test Ted to see if he would appreciate her artistic passions, so she persuaded him to tour the Iowa City Art Museum with her. He barely tolerated it. He did not seem to understand the art very well, but he admired Lorelei's translation of French titles and explanations of the milieu artists.

Lorelei tried to break off their Sunday afternoon dates. She certainly did not like the fact that he tried to kiss her goodbye.

Ted always misunderstood. Lorelei tried to arrange a dinner with him and older faculty members, and two nice women their ages, but at the last moment, the women pulled out, so Lorelei had both men for supper, and Ted made it very clear that <u>he</u> was the one dating her and not the faculty member. Clearer than she intended. When she wrote a note later trying to break it off with Ted, in response, she received a knock at her door, and the delivery of eleven roses from the local florist. Of course, Ted had ordered twelve, but she did not have the heart to tell him that only eleven had been delivered, and of course, being polite, she had to thank him.

The Sunday before Lorelei was to leave for her excursion, they drove up to the Dairy Congress in Waterloo. Ted confided: "Now, this is the way to spend a Sunday!" She was mildly interested in seeing the horses, never having seen any racing like that before. But the thing that bothered her the most that day was his terrible driving. He drove his

Old Chevy, as if it were a tractor, only fifteen to twenty miles an hour, and all over the road. Lorelei insisted that the only way she could survive the trip was to get behind the wheel herself. She thought to herself: "I used to grit my teeth anytime I got behind a slow *little man with a hat* driving along the highways, and here I am riding with one! I just have to get at least one *little man with a hat*, off the road!"

The day before her flight to New York to join the teenagers for Europe, Lorelei realized she had gained great respect for Ted. His forthrightness and honesty were impeccable. It was so good to know someone she could trust. She thought of marriage with him and knew instinctively that she would never have to be concerned about his getting interested in someone else, as Fred had done, and that was so important to her. So, that afternoon, Lorelei knew a proposal was coming when Ted drove her down to Mt. Union to see his farm. She was wearing casual jeans and a comfortable, peach blouse and matching peach bonnet. She got out and looked at the dark black soil. She remembered her father saying that black soil was the richest and best in the world, and the idea began to play on her how delightful it might be to live on a farm and see things grow and be married to an honest-to-goodness farmer. She also realized that she loved all types of animals, and the idea of raising sheep was appealing to her. She already knew that she felt no romantic magic with Ted, as his kisses were sloppy and wet. She also knew she would probably never have that type of love again, as she had with her Fred. She even admired the funny, blue-jean overalls that Ted was wearing, with his thermal red shirt sticking out of his thick waistline. He was not handsome, but he was cute, and his cheeks looked as if one would want to pinch them. He was his typical self that day, and yet, Lorelei could tell he was a bit nervous about something.

So, not thinking of any good reason to say no, when Ted stopped and looked into her eyes, she saw his pleading eyes in return. The question came in that low, gruff Iowan voice: "Lorelei, I love you and need you. Will you be my wife?" He took something out of his pocket, opened the black case, and presented her with a simple cut, one carat diamond ring. Lorelei assented: "Yes, Ted, I am intended to love you, too, and I will marry you. The ring is very pretty, and I will wear it. However, remember that I am leaving to tour Europe and will be gone for three months, so perhaps we should not make any wedding plans until I return." Ted was not sure what she meant by that remark. He confirmed nervously, "Nothing will change how I feel about you. Your Iowa farmer will be waiting for you."

Chapter Five:

European Tour with the Teenagers

(The Cruise)

Amid the ambience of pre-arrangements for the August Woodstock Music Festival, hippies stopped traffic for miles leading to the docks that first day in June, 1969, in New York City. Lorelei had purchased four cruise tickets several months in advance and made reservations at youth hostels. She was not sure yet which country would be the final tour, so she decided she would buy the airfare tickets in August. It was part of the funds that Lorelei had saved from her divorce settlement, and she had planned to return to Europe with at least one relative and two students. So, Lorelei, her nephew, David, and two of her advanced students, Stewart and Lara, boarded the MS Amsterdam Cruise ship that would take them to Nantes, France. Lorelei was their matriarch, an attractive middle-aged woman, with shoulder-length curly brown hair, medium height and weight and adventurous eyes. David was seventeen, weighed about one hundred fifty pounds and was five-foot seven. He had the beginnings of hippie-length red hair, a touch of freckles and similar rosy cheekbones to his aunt's. He had a German nose and a lighthearted disposition. Lara also had red hair, but hers was long and silky with medium-set hazel eyes. She was slim and tall, with a Roman nose and had a very shy disposition. Stewart, was somewhat opposite with straight brown hair, large walnut eyes, lanky physique, Grecian nose and a studious disposition. The teenagers brought their own spending money for food, exhibits and souvenirs. The boys wore khaki pants and casual short-sleeve shirts, and the ladies wore cotton dresses and cashmere sweaters to acclimate to the changes in Summer weather they would encounter. The trio was eager to hear of Lorelei's previous European experiences, as they had never been on a cruise before and were anxious to see the places she had planned for them: France, Switzerland, Italy, Monaco, Austria, Germany, Denmark, Holland, Belgium, Sweden, Amsterdam, England and Scotland. They were going to rent a car in Italy. The driving age requirements were a little different in Europe, so Lorelei would be the driver, although the trio hoped she might let them test drive just a little anyway.

Across the Atlantic, they ate like kings and queens and met other students from various countries, who had been exchange students in America. They shared their stories. Lorelei wore her simple engagement ring, but secretly whispered to her teenagers that she was not in total commitment yet.

She did not want to feel tied down on what might be her final European visit! The trio was often embarrassed by Lorelei, as she would dramatically introduce them. She would shout in a musical tone: "This is my nephew, David, from Georgia, and these two beautiful creatures are Lara and Stewart, my advanced drama students from Iowa!" The trio tried their best to hide behind each other when they knew introductions were coming! It was comical, especially when David would respond in his southern accent, lovingly: "Ya'll, this is my eccentric Aunt Lorelei! She was born in Michigan but lived as a rich lady in Boston!" Everyone laughed at his accent. On the cruise ship, especially in the evening for dinner and theatre, they always dressed their part. Lorelei would wear a different colorful pleated skirt and silk blouse each evening, always with a scarf to match, with never too much makeup or jewelry. She was the part of elegance, not too gaudy or too extravagant. The American teenagers dressed in their finest Church clothes. Lara dressed similar to Lorelei with just a touch of makeup for her olive skin, a colorful bow for her red hair, and a cotton skirt and blouse. Neither Lara nor Lorelei wore high heel shoes but rather satin ballet-type shoes for comfort. David and Stewart wore dark, polyester pants, white starched shirts and usually a tie to match with a suit jacket. They made for a nice-looking group that caught the eye of many tourists.

Lorelei and her teenagers were assigned to a dinner group, totaling twelve people that dined with them for each meal. Of the eight at their table, not counting themselves, seven were from seven different countries including Japan, China, France, England, Germany, Russia and Italy. The eighth dinner partner was a particularly, attractive German gentleman who immediately was able to converse with Lorelei, since she spoke German fluently from her previous tour studies. Lorelei noticed that he always wore a custom-made suit and tie, and his hair was a deep, dark brown that rolled away neatly from his forehead. He was average weight and height, and some of his eccentric gestures reminded her fondly of her father's. He was a Vintner, so he talked about his family vineyards in Germany. One evening at the dinner table, she surprisingly discovered his name was Claude Flora, and as her maiden name was also Flora, she was able to recite to him the Flora names of descent. Claude cleared his masculine, deep German voice and disclosed their family connection: "My great, great grandparents were also Jacob and Nancy Flora from Maikammer, Germany!" He jumped up out of his seat and ran over to hug her and shouted: "! - Ach du meine Güte!" and acted as if they had known each other for years! It made for a wonderful eight-day trip for Lorelei, as they daily walked the deck together, ate together every meal and swam in the ship's pool together, when it wasn't raining. They would always join the teenagers every evening in the entertainment theatre!

On the sixth evening, in the theater, they were sitting at a small table in the front row, facing each other in conversation and waiting for the magician to begin, when David blurted out to Claude: "Schaue hinter dich!" Claude was so shocked that David had learned German words so quickly that he did not look behind him in time and was greeted by the magician, who accidentally dropped the rabbit out of his hat on to Claude's head! Everyone laughed and laughed! The magician gave his apologies, jumped back up on the stage and began his magic show!

The week went by too quickly as everyone grew accustomed to each other and learned they had a lot in common. They enjoyed classical music, swimming, dancing, ping-pong playing on the deck and watching the porpoises in the ocean. Everyone took rolls of pictures with their Polaroid cameras. Lara was preparing for a

41

photography career and would organize her pictures immediately into her voluminous photo album. As he constantly poked fun at her, David sounded like a parrot: "Lara, that huge album is bigger than you!" She told everyone that she hoped to attend the private, Liberal Arts *Principia College* in Illinois. Lorelei interjected enthusiastically: "Oh, Principia College is very reputable, and I myself had always wanted to attend, but instead I went to Boston University, which was fabulous also!"

As the ship arrived in France, everyone rushed on deck to see the Gothic St. Cathedral Pierre and the Fortified Medieval Chateau of the Dukes of Brittany. Lorelei and Claude exchanged contact information, and he invited them all to his home in Germany. He rushed to Lorelei's side and reminded her: "I am divorced and have two daughters that I want you all to meet. They are the same age as David, Lara and Stewart. Remember, we have discovered that David is also a distant cousin! I am so excited to get to know you better!" Before Lorelei could respond, with both hands, he gently pulled her to his lips with a soft, slow kiss. Lorelei then hugged him in appreciation of not only the kiss but of their mutual discovery. As they prepared themselves for the captain's preparatory closing discussion, Claude and Lorelei continued to give each other giddy, farewell smooches. Lara, David and Stewart were feverishly embarrassed, looked at each other and shook their heads as they moved forward on deck.

(1. France)

Lorelei's previous exploits with the disembarkation process was extremely beneficial for the teenagers as she helped them through the long lines and crowds, as immigration officials performed their duties. After a long morning, they finally exited the ship in excitement and walked down the plank towards their awaiting adventures. Lorelei made arrangements for them to send correspondence to the U.S. She sent a postcard to Ted in Iowa, Lara and Stewart wrote to their families, and David wrote to his mom and siblings in Georgia to report their safe arrival. They exchanged some of their American dollars for francs and traveler's checks, as advised in the book that Lorelei had purchased in New York, Arthur Frommer's, <u>Europe on 5 Dollars a Day</u>. It included information of youth hostels that cost only fifty cents a night.

They took the train into Paris on a lovely lighted evening avoiding the daytime humidity. Lorelei told them they would be staying for three weeks in France, and she had made pre-reservations for them at the Le Montclair Youth Hostel, which was a little over budget, but special for their first tour. They would make it their home base and travel by bus. They would dress casual for comfort in the warm, sizzling temperatures of France.

Lorelei also had a special parlay for them. She asked each of them to provide a summary "theme" word for each excursion and suggested they have a final discussion together after each country's tour. She needed ideas for her writing journal, which she always had on-hand, because she wanted to write a novel someday about her experiences in Europe. They agreed that they would discuss their chosen words before travelling on to the next country. In addition to the theme word from each of them, they soon found out that Lorelei had a different adjective for each morning. On their first day, it was "beautiful," the second day it was "glorious," the third it was "marvelous." By the tenth day, David could not help but comment, "Aunt Lorelei, I did not know there were that many adjectives in the *English Dictionary!*" She just laughed in response: "I also can give you a song each morning to match that adjective!" The trio responded in unison: "No, no thank you, that is okay. You can just continue the adjectives!" Lorelei was in her element! She loved travelling in Europe! They shared her happiness!

They took a full-day city tour together by minibus and ate lunch near the Eiffel Tower. They purchased souvenirs from the many shops. Lara bought lovely Paris coasters for her mother. Lorelei bought a box of Paris stationary for herself. David bought an Eiffel Tower clock for his mother. Stewart bought an Eiffel Tower candle for his sister. They went on various excursions, including the art gallery and gourmet walks and bus guided tours of the Champs Elysees, Arc de Tromphe, Paris Opera, the

Louvre Palace (including the Egyptian Antiquities), the Orsay Museum and the Paris Islands. They also viewed Da Vinci's *Mona Lisa* and read the plaque below that noted it took Leonardo four years to complete. David pointed towards her smile and nudged Lara: "It looks like her smile shows that she was very tired of posing! She has a smirk on her face!" Lara rolled her eyes in response: "You are so silly! I see her smile, but when I look again, her smile has faded. What does it mean, Lorelei?" Lorelei responded in a serious tone: "From my studies, I have read that Da Vinci intended for the Mona Lisa to have that mysterious expression, so that the individual will use imagination to interpret."

Everyone found out early from their adventures that David was "the life of the party." When one least expected it, he pulled a prank. He was able to scare Stewart, his roommate, in the middle of the night at the window, as he had slipped out on to the terrace and scratched at the window, scaring Stewart out of his deep sleep. For Lara, one morning at breakfast, he switched his coffee cup for hers, when she was not looking, and she detested all the sugar he had in it! For his aunt, he would point to someone in the crowd and tell her it was an ole' American movie star that he knew she would love to see! She would run over to that person and find it was not; just someone David had made up for her!

David was able to converse with one of the street mimes using gestures and pointing. Lara wondered why he was pointing to her. Mimes usually stayed as still as possible and did not speak. However, David gave him a few coins to woo Lara, with a song. The white paint of his face and his stride towards her frightened Lara, and she started to back up. Then she saw that the mime had a pink carnation in his hand, and he was offering it to her. He drew his fingers together in a circle around her face in a type of sign language gesture to tell her she was beautiful. Lara could tell he was giving her a compliment by his genuine smile. Then to her surprise and to other tourists passing by, the mime sang one chord of Stevie Wonder's love song, *My Cherie Amour*. Lara then realized that David had paid the mime to woo her. She was a good-sport, shook the mime's hand and thanked him for his fine performance, and then ran to David and pretended to choke him in jest.

In their first, official theme discussion, Stewart was in awe of the: "Lights" as he shared his perspective of the multiple night lights of Paris. Lara quietly sighed: "Romantic" referring to the emotions of the lovers she saw in Paris. David pointed up to the stars: "Ominous" referring to how the Eiffel Tower reached to the sky. Lorelei summed it all with: "Shopping," referring to the mass numbers of souvenir shops and phenomenal Parisian scarves inside that she had wanted to purchase.

(2. Switzerland)

The foursome rode the train into Switzerland and stayed at the Zurich Youth Hostel. They took a bus tour and enjoyed the view of the snowcapped Alps and lakes. They visited the Museum Rietberg, which was renowned as the third biggest museum in Zurich, and the only art museum in Switzerland for non-European cultures. While studying the artworks from Asia, Africa and Oceania in the Museum Rietberg, Lorelei became separated from her teenagers. After about thirty minutes of frantically searching for them, Lorelei went down to the lobby to ask the information desk to page them. Lorelei was not thinking that they could have already walked outside. There was no response to her page. It was the first time that Lorelei felt such a huge weight on her shoulders. If something happened to those teenagers, she would be responsible. At that moment, she prayed they were safe. She had heard horrid stories of kidnappings in Europe of children their age. It also made Lorelei reconsider having such responsibility on a daily basis if she ever adopted a baby. Thirty more minutes went by, and Lorelei finally realized that they could have gone outside of the museum. She walked out and saw in the distance, a gazebo, where her teenagers, were sitting and sipping on Swiss beverages. She ran and scolded them. At first, they laughed at her for the foolish worry, but then saw how distraught she was, so they stopped laughing. They apologized and explained to her that they were just "shooting the breeze."

Upon their tour theme discussion, Lorelei spoke in relief: "My word for Switzerland would be *Thankful*, because I am so thankful that you are safe." Stewart spoke next: "My word for Switzerland would be *Apology* for making you stressful during this tour." Lara and David both nodded and David continued: "We also would choose the word *Apology* for the stress you experienced. You have been so kind to invite us on this European tour, and we should have made sure we stayed together, or at least told you we were going outside. Please forgive us." They all hugged, and David mimicked: "group hug," as was done in the American cartoons!

(3. Italy)

From Switzerland, they rode by train into Italy, where Lorelei rented a yellow European Volkswagen. The drive between Pompeii and the Amalfi Coast (Sorento) was spectacular! They were told by the Amalfi townspeople that there were about 1600 curves! For 50 miles, there were overhanging cliffs from start to finish. The terraces were steep with orange, lemon, olive, carruba and fig tree orchards clinging to the hillsides. It was the most breathtaking and peaceful emotion that Lorelei had ever felt in her life, and she sighed: "Home in my heart." Even the teenagers were amazed at the beautiful vistas! As they came into focus of the nearby Island of Capri, Lara was the first to capture photos. Lorelei told her teenagers in her most serious, dramatic tone: "I could just stop the trip right now and become a permanent resident!" Lara agreed, as she continued to take lovely photos from a distance. Stewart and David also rolled down their windows to take pictures, and in jest, beseeched: "Please, don't! We would like to continue our trip!"

As Lorelei was driving around the final 1600th curve and entered the roundabout, she gently bumped into another car. She cried, "Oh my golly! I hope I can speak their language!" She got out first and told the teenagers to stay in the car. She straightened her pleated white skirt and made sure her sheer, gray short-sleeve blouse was buttoned to the top and tucked in. The driver of the other car emerged, but his Italian was a little different from Lorelei's Italian studies. She was about to give up communicating her apologies, that it was only a small scratch, when another man arose from the passenger side. He was tall and tanned with black, perfectly combed hair, about age fifty and had the striking resemblance to the debonair movie star, James Bond. He was wearing crystal white suit pants and a starched, gray short-sleeve shirt unbuttoned enough to reveal traces of dark furry hair on his broad chest. He took off his dark sunglasses and introduced himself in English in a smoky, sexual tone: "I am Humberto, and this is my brother, Simone. We accept your apology and see no reason to write a report." All of a sudden, they both realized they had met each other five years ago at the *Commedia dell'arte* Italian Comedy Theatre! Lorelei was the first to clarify: "Are you the Italian gentleman I met at the the *Commedia dell'arte?*" Humberto nodded his head and looked into her sparkling eyes: "Yes, but at that time we did not have the pleasure to discover each other's names." She responded in her most dramatic voice: "I am Lorelei, named after "The Lorelei" in Germany! Have you ever seen *My Rock?*" Humberto eagerly responded, "Yes, I love that *Rock!* The legend is so mysterious and enchanting!"

After introductions, Lorelei adjusted the conversation back to the accident, by applying a soft-spoken voice: "Thank you so much for not pursuing an accident report. I have three teenagers with me. We are on tour here in Italy and have rented this car, so I deeply appreciate not involving the *Polizia di Stato*, so thank goodness there is only a scratch on your brother's car." Humberto smiled with his immaculate white teeth and reached for Lorelei's hand to kiss it in a friendly Italian gesture. His brother bowed in approval and returned to the driver's seat. Humberto then walked over to Lorelei's rental car and introduced himself to David, Lara and Stewart. He asked them questions about their tour and hoped they were having a good time. David was the first to speak in humor: "We just had a maniac drive the 1600 curves of the Amalfi Coast, but we are alive!" It drew a quick laugh from Humberto, but Lara and Stewart were not sure that David's wit was appropriate, since Lorelei just ran into their car. They did not know about the scratches. Lorelei came up beside Humberto with a spark-like touch to his arm and made sure the introductions were given. She was proud of her teenagers and said something complimentary about each one. He in turn was genuinely pleased to have met them. Lorelei could smell his relaxed scent of Italian citron cologne. He must have felt or heard her sigh, as he opened the car door for her and handed her his business card. Humberto looked into Lorelei's beautiful emerald eyes, and she looked into his, seeing a reflection of herself. He begged her to give him a call, whenever she was in Italy again. His business card noted that he was an Italian Art Collector. Lorelei smiled back with her best, sincere smile, and told him she hoped they would meet again. The teenagers were staring at the two of them, when Lorelei hurriedly asked them for a piece of paper, so that she could give Humberto her school phone number. She tried to hide her simple engagement ring that she suddenly remembered was on her left finger. Humberto did not seem to notice. Lorelei did not see a ring on his finger and wondered if he was still married to the young blond she saw him with five years ago. She thought of asking him of his marital status, but knew it would be inappropriate. So, they said their farewells: Humberto's farewell "Arrivederci" was tender and softly spoken. Her farewell "Perhaps we will meet again someday" was a matching soft-spoken, lingering goodbye. He waved to her teenagers, helped Lorelei into her rental car, and she watched him out of the corner of her eye walk back to the passenger side of his brother's car. David directed the trio with the Jay and Americans' song, "This Magic Moment," and asked: "Aunt Lorelei, were you flirting with that Italian stranger?" Lorelei answered her nephew's question with the story of her and Humberto's brief acquaintance in '64, and how coincidental it was that they had met again because of an accident. She explained she was not really flirting, just reciprocating his Italian kindness, the kindness that was so common among good-looking Italian gentlemen. David responded, "Looks to us like you were flirting! But, yeah, you'll probably never see him again!"

As Lorelei drove on towards Rome, and the teenagers were napping, she thought about Ted's proposal back in Iowa. Lorelei enjoyed teaching drama and someday wanted to write a novel about home talent shows, but Ted would expect her to help with his sheep farm. He had over 200 acres and a house that was full of Cleo's antiques. The house would have to have major repairs; it did not even have a full bath. She really enjoyed Celia's company and would love to have her as a relative. However, Lorelei had also wanted children, and now she knew that unless she adopted, that was not going to happen. She thought of what beauty she had just witnessed at the Amalfi Coast and of the charming Italian man, Humberto. She also thought about Claude, whom she had met on the cruise ship. She remembered "Her Rock" in Germany. She asked herself quietly, "Am I being lured instead of luring? What if I have to choose only one love, and that love will affect the rest of my life?" It brought chills to her arms and a feeling of déjà vu!

The four of them reached Rome in the late evening, where the old lantern street lights glowed. Lorelei was so happy to see Rome again. Her impression was much more favorable than it had been in '64. In '64, she took a little cart, and the driver gave her a piece of candy which turned out to be liquor-filled. She remembered that she dropped everything and jumped out to wash off her hands and coat in the nearby fountain. But this time in Rome, it was one of the most pleasant of the large cities she had ever seen, and much to her surprise, she found herself preferring it to Paris, although if she were living alone, one of the cities in Switzerland, Germany, Scandinavia or England would probably have been her preference. One of the ideas she had been toying with, before she met Ted, was to become a professor in Europe, because of the great libraries, even though her heart swelled with pride at being an American.

Lorelei had made reservations for them at the Four Season Youth Hostel. They enjoyed Cappuccino prepared with espresso and a pastry in the mornings. They each tried the special Roman pasta dish "Cacio e pepe" at the Ristorante Cecio nearby and celebrated Lara's 18th birthday. The sound of Italian opera music reflected the aurora of greenish lights and enhanced their mood of celebration. Lara had changed and was not so bashful anymore. She made the best of every situation, whether good or bad, and was so thankful to be with them. She felt a lasting friendship developing and knew they did also. The trip was giving them a chance to cultivate their personalities and ambitions.

They visited some of the Catacombs, the one where Peter and Paul were almost buried until their bodies were re-buried by St. Peter's in Rome after Christianity was legalized by the Emperor Constantine. The Arch of Constantine was to the right of the huge Coliseum, where the lions ate the early Christians. The ruins, "Foro Di Traiano" were in the foreground. They took the half-tour of the Vatican Museums and the Sistine Chapel with all its great art work. They were thankful they could take photographs inside. They found American Express and their next Youth Hostel and saw the city on the old Roman Road called the Appian Way. They viewed miles of the old walls around Rome and the beautiful monuments and fountains. Lorelei's refrain was undeviating and pleasurable to hear: "Ah, the fountains, the statues, the gardens, buildings and hills! Listen, as I tell you the legend of *The Trevi Fountain*! It is the famous fountain, where you throw a coin over your shoulder to find out if you will have the good luck to visit Rome again!" Obviously, her coin had brought her good luck, because she was visiting Rome again! She remembered the numerous Latin markings and tried to read some of them to her teenagers. She told them that every statue had a history to it. They were very inquisitive and thankful for her expertise, and they knew there would be amazing, historical sites they would not have time to see. One example was the fishing village, "Vernazza" where they could have seen boat ramps and enjoyed sunbathing, but Lorelei had to tell them of its beauty, as they did not have time to see it in person.

The symbolic wealth of art was overwhelming, and Stewart especially liked the archaeological collections. They also witnessed the Sunken City of Venice and strolled in Gondolas by the famous canals. The Gondolier stood facing the bow and rowed with a forward stroke and then a backward stroke. Lorelei was able to converse with the Gondolier and translated questions to him from the teenagers. David asked if the job paid much. Lara asked if he enjoyed his job. Stewart asked if he had been rowing all of his adult life. The Gondolier appreciated their questions and translated back to Lorelei that he made enough to feed his small family, that he enjoyed his job, because it was outdoors, and that he had been a Gondolier for over thirty years, as his father before him. Lorelei also enlightened them with a little trivia: "The famous author, Mark Twain, visited Venice in 1867." Lara responded:"I wonder how he may have compared the Mississippi to the deep waters of Venice!"

Each postcard that Lorelei sent to Ted back in Iowa, she tried to highlight details that she thought he would have enjoyed, but she was not sure that a farmer such as Ted would have ever dreamed of traveling beyond his farm.

Off budget again, Lorelei treated the teenagers to scooters. They were called, "Vespas." They rode all over Rome. Each one had a shiny, black Vespa. It was one of the highlights of their visit in Rome, because they each felt free to drive with the wind in their faces and see the scenery from their own unique perspective. At the beginning of their scooter ride, they all noticed there was no animal control, because the domestic animals roamed freely. They had to carefully watch out for the animals, especially the dogs and cats. As they were dodging a couple dogs around one curve, there was one dog, a mixed collie mutt, with one-eye, that jumped on a particular bus. Lara was the first to see him: "Look at that dog! He is jumping on the bus, as if he does the same thing every day!" Then, near the end of their excursion, they noticed the same mutt jumping off the bus at the same spot. They figured he had probably made his local rounds for food, and then knew he had to get back on the bus to go home. It was very peculiar in comparison to an American dog. Only an American guide dog was allowed on the bus with its blind owner.

Trains ran frequently from Rome to the coastal city, Naples. It was also a great way to view the beautiful scenery. When they arrived in Naples, it was wash-day. All along the main streets, clothes were hung everywhere. David teased his aunt: "Perhaps we can add our laundry to their clotheslines. I don't think they would even notice the difference!" They all laughed at David, as they had on so many occasions. He had a way about him that was humbling. He did not laugh at his own jokes and did not realize he was so funny. The southern accent and slang words he used naturally were just unusual to the others and comical, and his demeanor was so carefree and loveable.

On their way back into Rome, they enjoyed one of the oldest, open markets, "The Campo Di Dei Floria," where they tasted samples of fresh fish and different fruits and vegetables. David bought a pocket knife called "Cantine Ettore Sammaro" from an old man selling it among his vegetables. Sometimes they had to pay coins to go to the bathroom, so they would purchase something from the proprietors in order to use their facilities.

By the end of the second week in Italy, they were off again driving the Amalfi Coast to return the rental car. They finally washed their rental car, found someone willing to tackle it, which had been so dirty, because Lorelei had parked the car under an umbrella pine tree, where pigeons had left their evidence. David reminded them, holding his nose in imitation of the head customs officer: "Remember how the custom officers all held their noses as we passed through, without even taking time to look at our passports?" They all laughed remembering the hilarious incident.

Since Lorelei had told the teenagers they could drive, she agreed they could each drive a couple curves around the Coast. So, they packed their bags, said goodbye to Rome, and Lara drove the first twenty minutes of curves. She was an excellent driver, and then pulled over to let Stewart drive. He drove very carefully around the next five curves. He stopped the car before the next roundabout, so that David could drive. None of them realized until they noticed the small art shops beyond the hill from the roundabout that they were in the same location as they had been when Lorelei had the minor car accident with the Italian brothers. All of a sudden, Lorelei cried, "Stop! Let us take a break here!" She pointed to the art shop. So, Stewart pulled into a parking spot on the hill. David suggested to Lara and Stewart that they should go find a coffee shop. Lorelei told them she would meet them there in a few minutes. They walked up the hill, and David and Lara raised their thumbs high in the air to encourage Lorelei's beating heart. She looked at her attire in semi-approval: white slacks, turquoise silk blouse and matching scarf around her neck. She timidly walked into the shop. She immediately saw the handsome Humberto in an ivory business suit to the right corner of the room, holding a rare Italian sculpture. He almost dropped it when he saw the lovely Lorelei. He walked briskly over to her and gave her a soft kiss on each cheek, welcoming her to his shop. He introduced her to his two assistants, one which was the brother she had bumped into a month ago. He asked her if she had time to have tea with him nearby and of course asked about her teenagers. She said they were taking a break at a coffee shop nearby. He said they would find them. So, he spoke Italian to his brother to take over the shop, and he and Lorelei stepped out into the brilliant Amalfi Coast sun. He held out his arm for Lorelei to lean on as they walked up the hill together, smiling at her, and she at him. She knew that the beauty and magic of the Coast was probably the reason for her flutters, but she felt as if she was in a fairytale. They found the trio in the Coffee Bar sitting at the patio overlooking one of the many vistas of the Coast. Humberto shook the boys' hands and kissed Lara on both cheeks as he had done Lorelei. Humberto told them that he wanted to take them to eat the best Sorrento Spaghetti Omelet they would ever taste in their lives at the Amalfi

Coast Italian Restaurant. He winked at Lorelei as he invited them. They were excited and hungry, as they all loved spaghetti, and said yes.

As Humberto promised, the spaghetti was the best they had ever tasted. The trio sat together at the front of the table to give Lorelei and Humberto a chance to sit closer together at the end. By the time they had finished eating, Lorelei and Humberto were laughing as if they were young teenagers again. It was wonderful seeing their guardian so happy. However, they were not sure what would happen next. They knew they had to continue traveling to deliver the rental car. David was shocked at what Lorelei proposed: "Humberto has invited us to stay with him at the Hotel Diana in Pompei and has offered to help us return the rental car. So, I suggested that perhaps you could drive, David, since it was your turn to drive the rental car, and I could ride with Humberto, as we follow you in his car." David nodded in a joke: "Yes, Aunt Lorelei,

I could do that. I will try not to be a maniac's nephew around the curves!" Lara and Stewart did not laugh at his joke, but they agreed to the arrangement, because they could see that Lorelei was happy. They all walked back down the hill to their cars. David buckled up ready to drive, with Stewart in the front to navigate, and Lara in the back praying. Lorelei discreetly threw her engagement ring in her purse, as she reached to get her writing journal, and skipped back to Humberto's car like a high school girl going to her first dance.

As they drove the many curves, David was constantly looking in his rearview mirror to make sure that Humberto was following. David was a little concerned that they really did not know much about Humberto. He said to Lara and Stewart: "He could be a thief, a kidnapper or worse yet, a murderer, and we have allowed Lorelei to ride in the car with him!" Lara and Stewart were also apprehensive, but responded together: "She will be okay."

Lorelei and Humberto talked of their childhood days, travel experiences and education. She talked of her doctorate with mixed feelings: "I received my Ph.D. in Theatre Arts, when I was in my late thirties, and my dissertation was about the Hôtel de Bourgogne. It was France's first public theatre of the pre-classical era, and its influence and development on French theatres and drama. However, my age created a few challenges, since that field was so limited. They still hired mostly male theatre directors, or either young females, just out of college. I was very discouraged, so I opted for teaching drama at the community college level." Humberto could relate: "Yes, I ran across a few challenges myself. I received my Ph.D in Art History from the University of Bologna, where I wrote my dissertation about the first millennium BC, of the time of diversity and constant cultural change in the Italian region, which was the foundation for the iconic Roman Imperial traditions! Alas, there were other graduate students competing with that crucial era, so I was almost rejected. It was a very stressful time in my life. But now, my brother and I bought our little shop, and we hope to gather artifacts from that time!" Lorelei exclaimed: "We have alot in common, you and I, in Fine Arts!"

We continued our conversation about children, and how we were both childless. She asked him about his first wife and his divorce. He told her that he and his wife grew apart, because his job took him out of town too frequently. He sadly told her: "I would travel four days out of the week and only be home on the weekends, and even then I was guilty of working on my inventory of art collections. So, it was my fault." Lorelei touched his shoulder, "Humberto, it always takes two to make a divorce. Perhaps, your wife could not adjust to that type of lifestyle, but I think if she had really loved you, she would have been more understanding of not only your job, but of your passion for it." He met her sympathetic eyes. Lorelei asked him, "Do you ever travel to the States?" He replied regrettably, "I have not had an opportunity to travel to the States yet, but I would love to see the Italian Art at the Guggenheim Museum in New York City someday!" Lorelei responded half-seriously: "I have always wanted to visit that museum also! Perhaps we could meet there someday!" Lorelei then told him of her heartbreak five years ago from her first husband, Fred. She began to have tears in her eyes: "Humberto, I really loved him. He was my high school sweetheart, and I thought the world revolved around him. I would have never in my wildest dreams believed he would have found someone else." Humberto reached over with his gentle hand to brush a strand of hair from her eyes. She surmised that she felt so comfortable saying anything to him, because he listened with his big, Italian heart. When he reached over and touched her hand, she felt electricity throughout her entire body.

She had never felt so much electricity before, even with her Fred. She was ecstatic and felt he was also. There was some type of magic in the air, and although this was only their second time to meet each other, Lorelei felt she already knew so much about him. It was almost like that with Claude, she thought, but he was after all her cousin, and Humberto was definitely not in that category.

When they found the entrance to the rental car, she began to feel guilty. She thought of Ted waiting for her on his sheep farm. What would he think of her now? What was she doing? Was she going to go through with this fairytale charade and go to the hotel with him? What had her Church morals taught her?

Humberto helped Lorelei out of the car, and walked with her to the return counter, as she signed the papers. He motioned with a wink to the teenagers to get into his car and wait for them. David, Lara and Stewart were hesitant to continue their journey with this stranger they hardly knew. He seemed friendly enough and had insisted on paying for their spaghetti dinner and was a gentleman in every way, but they still had an uneasy feeling about his pursuit of Lorelei. After all, David felt responsible for his Aunt Lorelei in the way she felt responsible for them. He would not want to go home to Georgia and tell his mother that Aunt Lorelei had an affair in Europe. Lara and Stewart felt the same. Lorelei was their teacher. They had to talk some sense into her. So, when Humberto and Lorelei came back to the car, the trio asked Humberto if they could have a word with Lorelei alone for a moment. He stayed outside his car and waited for them to talk inside with the windows up. David was the first to speak, "Aunt Lorelei, do you realize what you are doing? We do not know this man. He could put us all in danger!" Lara and Stewart nodded in agreement and had questions in their eyes as well. Lorelei calmly quoted from Alfred Lord Tennyson's poem: "It is better to have loved and lost, than never to have loved at all." "What?" David asked. "Are you sure you want to go through with this? What about your fiancé, Ted? Are we all going to be a part of this affair?" The word "affair" hit home to Lorelei. She hesitated, looked down, looked out at Humberto waiting patiently and made up her mind: "I have to make sure where my heart is and follow my instincts. I am not married to Ted yet. I even told him that we would not make wedding plans until I returned. You kids will not have to be involved. We will work out a plan, so that you will not know what I am doing or what the outcome may be. Trust me. Okay?" The trio held out their hands to grab Lorelei's and chimed: "We will trust you, Lorelei, to do the right thing, but please be careful." They all hugged their group hug.

Humberto, in the meantime, had his own mixed emotions. He had a hint that Lorelei was engaged in America and knew that he may be stirring up trouble by pursuing her.

He felt deeply for her and wanted to love her, but he did not want to push her if she was not ready. He also did not want to rush again into matrimony, as he knew his job was so important. And yet, he felt that Lorelei would be the type of woman who would understand, because art was one of her passions also. So he waited patiently.

Lorelei, with a grin, motioned for Humberto to join them. He opened the driver's door and put the key in the ignition. He stopped, "All is well?" Lorelei nodded, "Yes! Let us move on! It is a lovely day!"

About two hours later, they arrived at the Hotel Diana. Humberto insisted on reserving and paying for a room for each of them, as the landlord of the hotel was one of his art collection customers. Lara and Lorelei, David and Stewart had always bunked together, so this was going to be different for everyone. Even the rules were going to be altered, because of what Lorelei had said about her privacy. She told each teenager before going into their separate rooms that they could choose to tour outside of the hotel only within a few walking miles, and they each had to be back in their rooms by sundown. She expected a note from each at the front desk when they were returning to their rooms for the evening. She reassured them that she trusted them and respected their privacy and hers. They were to meet in the morning downstairs for breakfast and would be ready to go to the train station for their next tour to Monaco.

It turned out to be an evening that "stayed in Italy" and neither David, Lara, Stewart nor Lorelei ever talked about it. There was not the usual tour summary discussion of theme words for Italy. Only on the flight back to the U.S. would their individual secret thoughts of that evening be revealed.

The next morning they each arrived at the meeting place in the hotel and said they had already had breakfast in their individual rooms. Everyone looked somber and serious. Humberto drove them to the train station in silence. Only when they all got out getting their suitcases from the trunk, did Humberto speak to them. He pulled out a black bag from his trunk. He said he had been saving the gifts in his trunk, with the hope that he would meet them all again. He presented each of them a small Italian statue from his Collection. For Lara, he reached out for her hand and kissed it tenderly, as a father would, and presented her a statue of "A Young Maiden." To Stewart, he shook his hand and presented him a statue of an architectural Roman Column. For David, as he shook his hand also, he gave him a statue of the famous bust of David. For Lorelei, he paused. He looked into her eyes that reflected the ray of love and presented her with the statue of "The Mermaid and Her Lover Kissing." He then reached in to give her that final, sweet kiss of goodbye. They all said thank you to him, and Lorelei could not look back, as they parted.

Before their next tour to Monaco, they discovered Florence, the wonderful city for shopping. Florence was a homeowner's paradise where one could furnish their home with beautiful arts and antiques. Lorelei told Lara she would someday order antiques for her new life at the farm in Iowa from one of those shops. Lara agreed that many of her selections would brighten her home with good memories. In one of the print shops, Lara purchased a special photo print of the Amalfi Coast, a print from the town view of Positano. They also saw the famous paintings and statues in the Uffizi Museum and famous Cathedral.

They stayed one night in a palace that Mussolini had once provided for his mistress, which was renovated into a Youth Hostel. At first, they were a little disappointed that it appeared to be so crowded and disorderly. They had become accustomed to the electricity process in the hostels, in which the electricity went off at nine in the evening. There was hardly ever any hot water, especially at the nine o'clock cutoff in which the hot water turned immediately into very cold water. So, everyone knew they had to turn in fairly early in time enough to get their showers and be in bed by the time the lights went out.

In Mussolini's palace, it was the evening that Lorelei saved her nephew's life, and it elevated their relationship into more than just an aunt and nephew. It was late that evening, and although David had already had his shower before nine, he forgot to fill up the ice bucket. He had a habit of eating ice by his bedside, because the water was not as good as the ice that melted. He knew his way down the hall to the ice bin in the dark, so he did not carry a flashlight with him. About the same time, his aunt had also forgotten to get her customary ginger ale from the soda pop machine. She also felt she could see her way down the hall without a flashlight, as the full moon was shining through the palace side windows. Before she arrived near the ice bin and soda machine, she heard her nephew's voice: "Hey guys, no problem here. I know you want my wallet, but I did not bring it out in the hall

82

with me, but if you want to go to my room, I will give it to you." Lorelei heard an angry, Italian voice respond: "Dammi I tuoi soldi!" Apparently, they did not understand David's English. By the time Lorelei arrived at the corner of the dark hallway, she had to devise a plan quickly in her mind to save her nephew. She decided on the dramatic way. She crept up. From the top of her voice, she sang: "Al ladro!" She heard two young Italian guys murmur in shock to each other to get out of there. Lorelei's strong, soprano voice had frightened them so intensely, they dropped their weapons. By that time, other tourists with flashlights came out of their rooms to see what had happened. Lorelei went up to her nephew, hugged him and asked: "Are you okay? Did they hurt you?" David looked down at the knives intended for him, and he shook his head: "I can't believe they would've used those knives on me. I didn't even have my wallet with me! You saved my life, Aunt Lorelei, in your wonderful, erratic way! You are my Guardian Angel!" She responded, "You are like a son to me!" Arm-in-arm, they walked back to their rooms, nodded to the shocked tourists, and left the knives on the floor without getting their soda or ice.

Lorelei was too upset from her nephew's near-death incident to even mention it was her birthday on July 8th. David remembered his mother telling him that her birthday would occur during the European vacation, but she had not reminded him of the exact date. Lorelei had always told her sister that she did not believe in celebrating her birthday anyway, and Donna Marie suspected it was because of their mother. In addition to it being her birthday, David's incident created a late evening for them, as Lorelei told the story of her mother's disappearance.

"No one talks about it when we see each other. It has been nearly 30 years ago. David, your mother and I were just teenagers, and your Uncle Donald and Aunt Marty were only three and four. Our mother had excused herself to the movies. She did that often when she heard my father and me studying together. We were always studying for my passion was reading and studying, and my father's was also. He had just completed his bar exam and was just hired as a civil lawyer in a small firm in Detroit. Our mother somehow felt inferior, although she was still beautiful and not too plump for her middle-aged years. She never wore much make up or jewelry. She had a natural olive complexion and wavy, light brown hair that hung over her shoulders. People always said she was just the older version of me. She could also play the piano so soothingly, without reading the notes. That tragic day, she gave me a quick hug and told me she loved me but ignored my father, as they had recently quarreled, and then went over to Donna Marie, who was reading a comic book and hugged and told her she loved her. Donald and Marty were in front of the television, and she quickly gave them both a hug. She had done the same thing many

Saturdays, so no one thought anything unusual about their mother leaving them."

The teenagers were sitting on the bed together with their eyes glued to Lorelei. She was sitting on a chair in front of them. She took a deep breath, and then continued: "My father filed a "Missing Persons" report the next day. Of course, we were all in total shock. Just as the police investigated, Donna Marie and I re-traced our mother's footsteps back to the movie and to the park to see if she had walked there. They found no trace of her, not even a scarf or her purse. Our father stayed at home with the two young ones, and Donna Marie and I daily walked the areas in Detroit that we thought our mother had walked. For three months we searched, until the Winter snows stopped us. The detectives never found her body, and there were no accident reports for that day. I swore to Donna Marie that someday I would find her through my genealogy research process. There had to be an explanation. We could not believe that our mother was dead."

"Needless to say, the mystery of our mother put a damper on our siblings' childhood. We did not celebrate each other's birthdays. We only acknowledged we were a year older. Our father did his best to raise Marty and Donald alone. I moved out right after high school and married Fred. Your mother, as you know, David, was a senior in high school, fell in love with your dad and married him before graduation. She finished high school in the evenings."

After she finished her story, no one knew what kind of questions to ask or what to say to console her. They were in shock that so many years had passed, and still it was a mystery. She wept a little and confessed that her birthday had passed, and she was a year older and shared Ted's birthday post card. The next morning, Lara slipped out with money from David and Stewart and purchased a belated birthday gift in a Florence boutique. The teenagers presented Lorelei with a beautiful, turquoise wool scarf, a ginger ale and a chocolate candy bar.

(4. Monaco)

By July 15th, they were on the train viewing the Mediterranean Sea. Lorelei shared the memories of her tour in '64 of swimming and basking in the sun. Her voice sounded so soothing, as she told them: "There were days on end that I would lay for hours on the milky, white sand and gaze at the clear, blue sea and greenery around me. I came to realize then my favorite color, turquoise, was the blend of pale blue and green, the symbol of eternity. I would close my eyes and hear the slap of the waves against the shore that never missed a beat and the symmetry of foreign voices. I felt like I was in heaven." David, Lara and Stewart were mesmerized as always when Lorelei shared her memories.

They visited the Prince's Palace in Monaco, and Lorelei informed them it was on the top list of the world's greatest attractions. They rode to the Palace on a bus around hairpin turns through the city. They climbed up a little narrow street. There they discovered a spectacular view of the city, the sea and surrounding mountains from the grounds around the Palace. In the Palace tour, Lara pointed to the amazing broche-like ornaments.

To get to the beach, they had to take another bus that winded down yet another narrow street through a tunnel. Lorelei told them it reminded her of the very unusual, narrow and steep streets of San Francisco. The beach was everything that Lorelei had told them it would be. David buried Stewart in the sand, and Lara built a huge sand castle and pretended her knight in shining armor was buried there. David pulled another prank. He knew his Aunt loved ginger ale. She was still striving each day to meet her goal of only spending five dollars a day in Europe, so she would buy a bottle of ginger ale one day, drink only half of it, and then the next day, she would mix it with a bottle of orange drink. So, David bought a bottle of root beer, and as she was basking in the sun, he poured half of it into her half-filled ginger ale bottle. When she woke up from her nap on the beach, she reached for her two bottles to mix the orange into the ginger ale and found the ginger ale full, so she assumed she had already blended them. She took a sip. The taste was horrible! She hated the taste of root beer! She looked at the full orange bottle again. It was perplexing, but then she remembered her nephew's previous pranks. In the distance, the trio were swimming and laughing in the waves. She waved at them, as a good-sport would, and decided not to scold him. She would get him back! They all enjoyed a wonderful afternoon in the sun.

At one of the Monte Carlo restaurants, they feasted on Mediterranean cuisine, which included yogurts and cheese, fruits, vegetables, olive oil and fresh seafood. Lorelei poetically murmured at dinner: "Monte Carlo is perched like an eagle's nest on a mountain by the sea! Ah me! It also reminds me of the Amalfi Coast!" The trio looked back at her and then each other and questioned her sighs. When David got up from his chair to go to the restroom, Lorelei plotted her prank. She asked Lara and Stewart to help her, and they were ready to oblige. David had pulled enough pranks on all three of them. So, Lorelei told Stewart to go personally to the chef and ask for a sample of raw oysters. She knew David detested them! She told Stewart that the chef would have to put them in something that David liked in order to cover them up. They would say it was the chef's special of the day, and everyone would act like they were going to eat it also, but they would just pretend. So, Stewart asked the chef to conceal it in macaroni and cheese, David's favorite dish! When the chef brought it to the table, Lorelei suggested that David try the special first. David exclaimed: "Oh, yes, I love mac and cheese! I will try it!" He took a big portion on his plate, to his mouth, but stopped in mid-air, as he saw Lara smirking suspiciously! However, he did not catch it in time, it went down his throat, and he screamed: "Help! I just swallowed something very raw!" Even others around them laughed! David knew then that he had been taken. He choked, "Okay, we are even now! No more pranks, agree everyone?" They all nodded in agreement.

In their tour theme discussion, they always took time to share their photos. Sometimes they would swap and give away a photo to Lara who loved additional photos for her album. David was the first to provide his theme word with enthusiasm: "Lucky" referring to Lorelei's choosing him to go on the trip instead of his older brother, Steve, who was asked first and could not go. Lara went next and with her rolled tongue smiled: "Cuisine" referring to the great selection of foods they had eaten. Stewart explained: "The Galleries" of the double-decked galleries that impressed him. Lorelei reminisced: "Ah, Memories," of swimming in the Mediterranean Sea and of her private, unspoken adventure.

(5. Austria)

When they next arrived in Austria, they decided to cancel their reservations with the youth hostel. They made a reservation at the Goldenes Theatre Hotel in Salzburg, even though it was a bit more expensive. The Theatre Hotel was much more convenient to the places they wanted to visit. They could walk to most of the historic and interesting points of the city, including Mirabell Castle and gardens, the theaters, the churches and museums, the Congress House, the Central Train Station and to the famous "Old Town Centre" with its historic buildings and monuments. Stewart especially appreciated seeing the famous baroque architecture of "Old Town." They also took the tour of the city where the popular musical, *The Sound of Music*, had been filmed in 1965. They had of course seen the musical several times back home.

They took the "Salzburg" day trip and saw the birthplace of Mozart. The weather was perfect within the alpine mountain setting of magnificent gardens. They loved listening to Vienna's musicians. The Salzburg Festival that had been established in 1920 and was held each Summer for five weeks in late July was not quite underway, but they saw preparations for the big event.

That evening, they attended a dark comedy play, where David happened to hear during *Intermission* that three rows behind them was sitting the Chancellor of Austria, Josef Klaus. Comically, they all tripped over each other, as they hurried back to their seats to get a glimpse of him. Lorelei knew a little about him, that he was a Christian, Conservative politician. He gave them a kind smile with his dimple chin and nodded, when he saw them staring at him. Lorelei waved. The three of them were so embarrassed by her wave. They shrunk down into their seats. The lights were turned down for the final act.

Upon their tour theme discussion, Stewart provided the word "Glamorous," referring to the palace chandeliers. Lara provided the word "aroma" referring to the lovely smell of the flowers in the gardens. Lorelei noted: "Musical" in tribute to all the beautiful music. David provided "trumpet" referring to the jazz musicians. He pretended to play his own trumpet and sang his rendition of Louie Armstrong's *Hello Dolly*. They all clapped at how much he really sounded like the famous jazz singer.

(6. Germany)

By the time they arrived in Germany, it was the end of July, and Lorelei received a letter from Ted. He wrote about the monumental event that occurred on July 20, 1969, the Apollo 11, where Neil Armstrong was the first man to walk on the moon's surface and communicated by phone to President Richard Nixon. Ted also wrote kind words: "Lorelei, I miss you so much and love you. I have a surprise for you when you return!" Lorelei took a deep breath after reading his letter, said a little prayer and shared her letter. Of course, they had been able to watch the historical event from the television set at the youth hostel, but hearing again of America's news, everyone felt nostalgic and missed their families. For Lorelei and David, Germany was their ancestral home, and Lorelei was determined to find out more through the ancestral hometown tours guided by travel experts.

Stewart and Lara chose to take a steamer boat down the Rhine River to see "The Lorelei," while David and Lorelei arranged to see their cousins. David reminded Lorelei that Claude had invited them to his home in Maikammer. So, Lorelei immediately contacted their Cousin Claude, and he was true to his word. Claude picked them up from the train station in casual brown slacks and a handsome, tucked-in dark brown polo shirt that embellished his almost-perfect physique. He complimented Lorelei's beauty in her casual gray slacks and dark gray cashmere sweater that revealed her perfect curves. Her hair was wavy in the German breeze, and her small diamond ear rings glittered. David wore a dark, blue turtle neck and brown leather jacket that resembled Steve McQueen's detective attire in his movie, *Bullitt*, except for the red hair.

Claude's daughter, Hanna, greeted them at the door. Hanna was slender and beautiful, with long dark brown hair and dark eyes that portrayed the descendant of a lovely maiden of Flora descendants. She was wearing casual jeans and a yellow silk blouse that brought a lovely compliment from David. In her sweet, German accent, she explained: "I am sixteen and hope to visit America soon as an exchange student!" David responded joyfully in his southern accent: "I met exchange students on the cruise ship and can share some of those stories with you!" She commented immediately that she loved his accent! She also apologized that they would miss meeting her sister, Babi, who was away at school.

Their servant escorted them into the family room, and David and Lorelei were offered tea and tea cakes. As David and Hanna talked of student exchange stories, Claude escorted Lorelei to a corner of the room. As they stood there, looking in each other's eyes, Claude spoke softly in his German accent: "I have missed you terribly, Lorelei. Is there any way that we can see each other again on your tour? Can you share your schedule with me?" Lorelei responded in a low voice: "Yes, we are heading towards Denmark, Holland, Amsterdam and Belgium in a few days. Is there any place we could meet?" He responded with euphoria: "Yes, I have wine business in Amsterdam scheduled in two weeks, but I can re-schedule to match your time there. Let us set a date and a place!" He wrote down her contact information of their hostel in Amsterdam and told her he would call to confirm.

The afternoon went by too quickly. Claude and Hanna walked David and Lorelei to the door. David asked Hanna if it was possible to choose his family for her upcoming host family. She said she would inquire about the possibility. So, he gave her his mother's phone number and address. They hugged each other as cousins, and Claude and Lorelei walked hand-in-hand back to his car, where he would take them back to the station. On their drive back through Maikammer, Claude provided the hometown tour Lorelei had wished for, and he was a marvelous replacement for the travel expert, as he was able to match surnames to their ancestor origins. It was like driving back in time hundreds of years ago. He told them of a few descendants who still owned the family vineyards, besides his family. He blurted out surnames: Harter, Eller and Beigler! Lorelei pulled out her journal book, where she kept a copy of her family chart in the zipper department. She exclaimed, "Claude, those surnames are on our family tree!" He stopped the car beside the green hills to study her family chart. He was impressed with her research, and her beautiful handwriting of the family names. He gave her a tidbit that he was not sure she knew. He said, "Each of us has the exact same handwriting style as one of our ancestors. Sometimes, we just never found out who that ancestor was." Lorelei again was enthralled with Claude's similar passion for family research. In pure delight, she responded: "I did not know that! Now, I have something else to research!" He also said, "Your handwriting reflects how beautiful you are, inside and out." She blushed. He continued to tell them as much as he could and only wished they had more time, so they could visit some of their cousins' homes. He promised to give her addresses, so she could at least write to them in the future for more genealogy information.

Time ran out, of course, and Lorelei and David both thanked him profusely. At the train station, Claude gave Lorelei a lingering, long tender kiss and held her close. It reminded her of Humberto. David noticed how Lorelei looked into Claude's eyes and wondered what she was looking for. Lorelei had not told Claude about her engagement and did not think it was necessary. They would meet again. They waved goodbye.

Back at the hostel, they shared stories and photos. Lorelei and David described the architecture, especially to Stewart, who was thinking of studying architecture at Frank Lloyd Wright's School of Architecture. They described Claude's brick home of three stories and grand entrance adorned with transom windows. It was a fine example of German wealth from the family-owned vineyards. From their tour, Lara and Stewart told of sampling those family wines from the Rhine Valley region.

In their official theme discussion, Lorelei was the first to express satisfaction, when she said: "Roots," as she referred to Claude, the expert, who showed them their paternal roots. Stewart provided the word "Refreshing" as he referenced the Rhine River. Lara provided the word "Intriguing" as she referred to "Lorelei's Rock." David was smitten by Hanna, so his theme word was the phrase: "Spirit of Infatuation."

(7. Denmark)

When they arrived in Denmark by train, they went straight to their youth hostel and planned the next day's festivities. They were off to Copenhagen City on the hop-on-hop-off tour to see towers and turrets and "The Little Mermaid." Lorelei told them of the similarities to *Her Rock* on the Rhine and how "The Little Mermaid" also represented the Spirit of Love, except that the mermaid was a fairytale about a Copenhagen ballerina. Their hostel was close to City Hall Square, to the longest pedestrian shopping street in the world, Strøget, where cars were prohibited. Danish souvenirs were off budget but too enticing. Lorelei purchased a small Royal Danish Porcelain butter plate, Lara bought a bracelet from Tiffany of Copenhagen, David purchased a Danish design yellow flower for his mother, and Stewart bought a set of LEGO blocks that was designed in 1949 from Denmark.

A special highlight in Copenhagen was the *Tivoli Gardens*. Lorelei was very familiar with the story. She told them that the *Tivoli Gardens* had opened in 1843 and was one of the most popular theme parks in Europe. She had once read in Disney's biography that he had modeled *Disneyland* after *Tivoli*, because he had once experienced its magic also. The park was known for its quaint charm and captivating themes. There were many attractions, gardens and restaurants, including a wooden roller coaster. The teenagers wheedled Lorelei to ride the roller coaster with them. Lara and Stewart sat together, and David sat with his aunt, as she closed her eyes the entire ride, but confessed when the ride ended: "Ah, but it took my breath away!"

In their theme discussion, Stewart provided the word "Turrets" referring to the castles. Lara provided the word "Innocence" referring to the mermaid. David provided "Exhausted" as he referred to jumping off and on the tour. Lorelei summarized with the theme word "Fairytale" by reciting from memory, another story, *Princess and the Pea* by Copenhagen's famous author, Hans Christian Andersen.

(8. Holland, Amsterdam and Belgium)

They combined their tours of the Netherlands. They experienced the Lindbergh Tour and saw the unique, colorful tulips and tasted amazing Holland chocolates. They toured the Anne Frank House and were lucky to do so, because it was scheduled for renovations the next year. They discovered a festive Dutch restaurant in Aruba, which served various samplings of Brussel sprouts, Belgian endive, sauerkraut, rookwurst sausage, Dutch coffee and tea.

In Amsterdam, Lorelei received a phone message at the hostel from Claude. She returned the call, and he told her he would be able to meet her at the Violala. He did not tell her what the Violala was, but he suggested she bring along her teenagers. They were all delighted that it was an ultra-modern bowling alley, where college students were having a bowling disco. They were also thankful they had worn comfy casual jeans for bowling and brought socks for the rental of bowling shoes. Lorelei had on a bright red t-shirt with the label of the U.S. flag, and Claude wore a bright green t-shirt with the label of the flag of Germany. When they chose teams for bowling, they joked about their competitive shirts, and David, as bowling captain, put them on separate teams. Lorelei and Claude bowled a few games with the teenagers, and then excused themselves to the seating behind them to watch. Lara and Stewart were very talented bowlers, but could not beat David's high scores. He bowled almost 200 every game. They even took a short break to do a little disco dancing with the other college students. Lorelei and Claude laughed, as they watched the teenagers point to their toes, then point upward to the ceiling, and both trying to dance with Lara at the same time. They agreed that the Old German Waltz was their kind of dancing.

At nearly ten o'clock, Claude suggested they have ice cream on the way back to the hostel. They enjoyed the chocolate frozen "yoghurt." Stewart, Lara and David felt the warning sign again that Lorelei was planning a rendezvous. Claude dropped them off at their hostel and waited in the car for Lorelei. She walked her trio inside and bade them good night, that she would see them at breakfast in the morning. David felt confident that his aunt was just having a casual date with a distant cousin, so he nodded his approval and ushered the other two up the stairs and said good night. Lorelei returned to Claude's car, got inside and was ready for a German escapade.

Claude took Lorelei on an evening stroll along the canals and crossed the historical bridges. Lorelei felt safe and secure with Claude, as they walked and talked about their ancestors. She felt like her great grandmother, back in time. He also told her something she did not know that impressed her: "I received my Master's in Business Management at the University of Hohenheim in Stuttgart. At one time, I wanted to go all the way, as you did, but I found the work so overwhelming, I did not have the time to continue my graduate studies." Lorelei had never even thought to ask him about his education. She boldly asked: "Claude, are you also a Christian?" He had not meant to laugh, but he did: "Of course, I am a Christian! My wine business would not be as successful as it is, without my Faith."

They stopped to sit by the water, and Claude touched her hand and looked into her eyes. He lifted her face to his, and they kissed tenderly. As they kissed, Lorelei could not help comparing. Humberto's kisses had been passionate, Ted's had been turbulent, and Claude's kisses were like nostalgic moments in time. It was difficult to analyze, but she was grateful for the opportunity to choose. Claude said tenderly to her: "Lorelei, you are a *hubsche Frau* and so vivacious. We are kindred spirits. Do you think that you could love me as I am loving you?" Lorelei looked into his eyes, and then she told him: "Claude, if this had been another day in time, I would not have hesitated to follow your love. However, I must tell you I am engaged to a farmer back in Iowa, and I must proceed with that commitment." Claude looked down at their hands entwined and shook his head: "Lorelei, I do not think I understand as I should, but I have to honor your decision. I hope that we can remain friends and cousins, of course, and that you will invite me to your wedding?" Lorelei was so touched and thanked him in earnest. She silently mused: "I have been given two offers, so far, in Europe. I am a lucky girl, or am I?"

Lorelei confided to the teenagers of her evening with Claude. She told them of his kind words, but she did not reveal her comparisons to Humberto. She told them that she was humbled but felt that the European trip was tempting her decision back home. Lara comforted Lorelei, "Your heart and faith will help you make the correct choice." Stewart asked her, "Is Claude a Christian?" David added, "Yes, and was Humberto a Christian?" Lorelei only knew that Claude had relayed that information. It had not seemed important to Lorelei at the time, but her teenagers brought up a very crucial credential.

Upon their tour theme discussion, David tried to sound humble with his word "190" referring to his bowling average, and they laughed with him. Stewart's word was "Phenomenal" referring to the windmill tour at Lindbergh. Lara's word was "Delicate" for the beautiful tulips. Lorelei's word was "Sad" for Anne Frank's tragic life, thinking again of her own mother's life. Was her mother still alive? If so, where was she?

(9. Sweden)

Their next focus tour was in Sweden where Stewart coaxed them into taking the Stockholm Ghost Walk and Historical Tour of medieval stories. They enjoyed a mystery play that evening, and Lorelei encouraged Stewart and Lara to take notes for their drama classes back in Iowa.

They enjoyed walking the streets in Sweden and witnessed the culture, mythology and folklore seen within their traditional, Swedish costumes. Lorelei and Lara each bought a little Swedish doll with flowers in her hair. Stewart and David each bought the little stuffed moose with the Swedish flag on his shirt.

The *Gustaf af Klint* steamship-turned-hostel was not only a bargain, but a unique hostelling experience. It was named after the Swedish, naval vice-admiral and cartographer, who was knighted in 1805. It was near Stockholm's Old Town and Metro. The rooms were Spartan-like, with porthole windows and bunk beds.

The hostel was near Skansen, the open-air Swedish Folk Museum and Park, where they celebrated the season of midsummer along with thousands of other tourists.

When they met for their theme discussion, David was first to provide his word, as he laughed: "Scary" referring to the ghost walk. He tried to explain to Lara that in her photographs, during the ghost walk, there were several "orbs," white dots, that represented the ghosts. Even the tour guide had mentioned the white dots. But Lara insisted it was just the way the light reflected at the time of the picture. Lorelei and Stewart agreed with her. They did not believe that ghosts would show up in photographs, but David continued to be skeptical. Stewart continued their conversation with his theme word "medieval," as he referred to the stories. Lara excitedly shouted: "Dramatic" as she referred to the play. Lorelei clapped her hands and shouted: "Historical," as she referred to what they had learned from their historical walk and steamship experience.

(10. England)

In August, they arrived in London, during the warmest month of the year. Lorelei had made reservations for them at St. Paul's Youth Hostel (YHA), where they would stay for three nights. The next day, she allowed choices for the teenagers, but insisted they always checked in at a meeting spot at Trafalgar Square by dusk. One day it rained all day, so their small-packed umbrellas came in handy. David, Stewart and Lara chose to see the Big Ben, St. Paul's Cathedral and Buckingham Palace, in spite of the rain. Lorelei chose to spend her time in the National Gallery and London Library. In the National Theatre Collection, she researched 16th century artists. Stewart was able to communicate the best with the Londoners; David and Lara enjoyed mimicking the English accents. At one turn, Stewart mysteriously excused himself and entered a nearby jewelry store. In the City of Westminster, they came together and celebrated David's 18th birthday at the Abracadabra Russian Restaurant at Piccadilly Circus. The entire staff came to their table and sang, *Happy Birthday* in Russian, *S dnem rozhdeniya!*

Lorelei shared with the trio a discussion of her studies from the London Library. She found an interesting article about England's rising problem in atheism in regards to Bertrand Russell, the British philosopher. He wrote about the concept of "teapot," in which it orbits the Sun somewhere in space between Earth and Mars. Russell's teapot "opened a can of worms" concerning the existence of God. Although, Lorelei rarely talked about religious issues, she could not help herself. She was opinionated: "Russell's ideas of freedom of thought are preposterous! What is this world coming to anyway? When people start questioning their faith, what will be next?" Stewart was the first to respond, "Lorelei, people have been giving their ideas for religious freedom for centuries. It will never change, but you are right, it may get worse." Lara questioned: "Wasn't Christianity founded in England?" David was quick to respond: "Yes, it was, and many of England's most notable buildings and monuments are religious in nature, such as the Stonehenge, the Abbies, St. Paul's Cathedral and Canterbury Cathedral! I agree with my aunt that philosophers like Russell will possibly influence more atheists to come forward!" Lorelei agreed that they should, then and there, say a prayer for the world, so they huddled to pray together.

In lieu of their usual tour theme summary, Lorelei had a surprise. Since they had not been able to tour Shakespeare's home at Stratford-Upon-Avon, she gave highlights of her visit there years ago. The surprise was acting out the play together: Shakespeare's *Romeo and Juliet*. Lorelei was Juliet's mother, Lara was Juliet, Stewart was Romeo, and David was narrator and imitator of all other parts. Lorelei and David sensed a genuine relationship developing between Lara and Stewart, as they watched them play their roles. David kept them constantly laughing, as he tried to imitate each character with a different voice and tone. They also queried Lorelei's constant sighs: "Ah me," as if she were either referring to their acting performances or to her lovers on tour.

(11. Scotland)

They took a bus to the Castle Rock Youth Hostel in Edinburgh's Old town. It was a 19th century palace-like building decorated with art and colorful dormitories inside. There was a cozy lounge with a piano and two large sofas by the fireplace. It was conveniently located about a ten-minute walk from Waverley Train Station, a three-minute walk from Grassmarket and Edinburgh Castle and a five-minute walk from Princes Street Gardens, The Scottish National Gallery and the National Museum of Scotland. Lorelei and her trio were able to spend at least an hour in each exhibit from the Grassmarket, historic market square to the National Museum's rich galleries of Scottish history and world cultures.

They took the boat tour of Loch Lomond and hiked in the Trossachs National Park. They rode in an open-top bus tour of Edinburgh, where David comically stood on the seat as if he was a stilt man marvel from *Marvel Comics* and took pictures of the ancient Edinburgh Castle. As she helped David back down to his seat, laughing at him, Lara captured additional ideas towards a career in photography. Stewart especially enjoyed the medieval fortress of Old town and neoclassical urban character of Georgian New Town.

After the tour, Lorelei made flight reservations for their return to the States. They were scheduled to fly out together on the last day of August from Glasgow, Scotland to the John F. Kennedy International Airport. David would fly separately back home to Georgia. Lorelei, Lara and Stewart would fly to Iowa.

In their final theme discussion, Stewart's word was "neoclassical" as he referenced the tour of New Town. Lara's word was "Walking" and Lorelei's word was "Wildlife" both referring to the nature walk and cute red squirrels at the National Park. David's word was "monster" as he referenced the legend of Loch Lomond.

Their final theme word together for their amazing adventures was "Family." They had created a distinct bond. They knew they would stay in touch as a close-knit family would. They each pulled from their pockets, small farewell gifts they had hid from the others and had bought from various shops on tour. They were in Lara and Lorelei's room, so they placed the gifts on the small table by one of the bunk beds. Since there were about 16 gifts, David suggested they each choose four. They were small items including magnets, charms, notepads, ball point pens and pencils. It was interesting to see who picked which item, just because of the country. It gave away which country they had picked as their favorite. Lorelei chose Italy and Germany items. Lara chose England and Scotland. David chose Denmark. Stewart chose Sweden. Yet, they all admitted they really loved every country they had been fortunate to visit.

(Flight Back to America)

On the flight back from Scotland, their individual, secret thoughts were revealed of that special evening in Italy.

Lara was sipping her tea and eating the airplane peanuts, as she thought about her secret evening in Italy. All three of them had gone out to eat at a nearby Italian bar. As they knew that Lorelei did not drink wine, liquors or beer, none of them had drunk on the tour, except for a little wine sampling in Germany, so they decided they would all try just one. Lara had a red wine and both the boys had a beer. They ended up having only a few appetizers, and as they talked of Lorelei and worried about what she might be doing, they drank a few more of each. By sundown, Lara told them they needed to get back to the hotel to check in and write the note to Lorelei that she had told them to write. David and Stewart agreed with Lara and thanked her for remembering. Lara wrote the note for each of them, saying that they had safely returned to their rooms and were going to sleep. However, it did not quite happen that way, as Lara sipped another sip and smiled up at the ceiling in the airplane.

She continued her thoughts: Stewart and David jokingly lured Lara into Stewart's room. Lara was relaxed after drinking her wine, and she suggested they put on some radio music. The room was then filled with music from the Beatle's, and one song she would always remember fondly was "All You Need is Love." Stewart reached for her hands, and they danced around the room. And then he kissed her slowly and sweetly. Lara had never been kissed before. She kissed him back and relaxed in his arms. David poked fun of them at first, in his witty way, but then he excused himself to his own room.

Stewart sat beside Lara in the plane and saw her smile. He thought that she must be remembering their secret evening together, so he reached over and took her hand in his. He knew at the moment that their college classes back in Iowa would be traveling a much different venue than before. He knew that she felt the same. He smiled back at her, and they both closed their eyes remembering.

David sat beside Stewart on the plane and saw that he and Lara were holding hands, and he smiled to himself. He was happy for them. They made a good couple. He thought about the secret evening in Italy. Before he went back to his own room, he was too curious and worried about his aunt to sleep yet, so he went downstairs to the lobby. He walked out to the parking lot and did not see Humberto's car, so he figured they had gone out to eat. He went back into the lobby, could not decide what to do, when he noticed a small library in an alcove to the left of the front desk. He discovered among the small collection of British writers, a wonderful play from Dublin's author, Oscar Wilde, *The Importance of Being Earnest,* so he decided to relax and read a little on the sofa in the lobby. He would wait for his

Aunt Lorelei to come in from dinner, so he could make sure she was safe. David glanced at the Italian Grandfather Clock on the wall above the counter, which ticked that it was not yet midnight. He sat back on the Volo white sofa, and soon the beers that he had consumed took the best of him. He remembered that he was in Act Two, laughing quietly at the antics of the main character, and must have fallen asleep, because when he woke up, he saw his Aunt Lorelei sitting across from him on an antique Vintage lounge chair, smiling.

Lorelei was sitting behind her teenagers by the window. She was quietly crying, thinking that her secret evening had gone exactly as expected. She and Humberto had opted to go to a quiet, romantic Italian restaurant a few miles away from the hotel. They wore their finest evening clothes, as if they were royalty. Lorelei wore a sheer, strapless, ocean blue evening gown that revealed just a little of her beating heart, with pearl earrings, matching gloves and a lovely pink shawl. Humberto wore a smoky, gray suit and tie. Lorelei had applied a touch of white musk perfume to intensify her emotions of sensuality. Humberto's scent was from Monsieur Worth's cologne of a fresh spice of wood. They shared a lovely Italian lasagna dinner, and Lorelei even drank a small glass of white wine, that she had never done before. She felt different and very relaxed that evening, as she knew it might be her last chance to ever experience such a romantic evening again. She tried not to think of Ted back home. She wanted to clear her mind for only Humberto. She knew he would be a perfect lover by the way he whispered sweet compliments. He would want to please her in every way. At dinner they did not talk about the future but only the present. In the background, the Italian opera of Shakespeare's *Midsummer Night's Dream* was softly playing. Lorelei knew that Humberto was trying to seduce her. She also knew that if she left that restaurant and went back to the hotel with him to his room; it would be the most magical night of her life. As they finished their meal and no dessert, Humberto made his move and looked into her emerald eyes: "Lorelei, *Amore mio, Ti amo.* You are the most beautiful woman I have ever met and you are *Anima mia.* Will you let me make love to you?" Lorelei looked back into his eyes with genuine love and murmured affectionately: "Humberto, you have already seduced me with your eyes, as your eyes are the soul to your heart. *Baciami!*" Humberto leaned over and kissed Lorelei passionately, tenderly and softly, all at the same time. Lorelei's entire body melted from his kiss and his touch. She had always dreamed of such a kiss, such a touch, and she could not even remember Fred's kisses at that point. He was a husband and a lover from another life. This was her life, that moment in time that so many lovers cherish. It was the ultimate, breath-taking feeling and peaceful emotion she had felt at the Amalfi Coast, where she felt "home in her heart." She was home with Humberto.

As the plane gave a jerk, Lorelei touched her lips with her right forefinger and smiled with a sigh: "Ah, me!"

The others had fallen asleep, so they did not notice. She closed her eyes and prayed for her future. She would leave it to fate.

Chapter Six:

A Lifetime Decision

Everyone arrived safely back to their families, David with his newly-grown red beard; Lara and Stewart with their new-found love; and, Lorelei, with her new-resolve. They would see each other again in the New Year at Lorelei's wedding.

Lorelei came back to a big surprise from Ted. When he picked her up at the airport, he hugged her so tightly that she thought he would burst her ribs. He told her he had a surprise waiting for her at the farm. About two miles from their arrival at the farm in Mt. Union, Ted made Lorelei wrap her scarf around her eyes. As they stopped, and he helped her out of the car, he whispered in her right ear that he loved her and hoped that she would be happy with his surprise. She took off her scarf and saw that the previous white-wooden two-story 1893 farmhouse had been painted a lovely, faded turquoise color, her favorite! She was very pleased. He said there was another surprise inside. He guided her to the back of the house to the master bedroom. The adjoining, previous, incomplete bathroom had been renovated to a wonderful modern full bathroom with all the conveniences that Lorelei would have ever dreamed. She was very thankful and murmured a quiet prayer to herself. She ran over to hug and kiss him, and he said they would celebrate and reunite over a pot of oyster stew that he had especially made for her return. She felt comfortable about her choice. She bragged about her teenagers and what fun they had. He asked no questions about anyone she might have met.

The next few months were busy for Lorelei. With help from Celia, they planned a small wedding ceremony for January, and Lorelei gave her notice to the college that she would teach only part-time in future semesters. She sold her Clinton mobile home and offered Ted payment for additional renovations for the kitchen and dining areas, but Ted told her to put her money in savings. She was able to order an Italian crystal chandelier and vase from the stores that she and Lara had seen in Florence.

Lorelei arranged for an auctioneer to appraise his first wife, Cleo's antiques. After the appraisal, she and Ted kept the few pieces that were appraised over a thousand, and sold the others in a yard sale, including the sale of a matchbook and postcard collection.

By 1970, the Vietnam War had taken the lives of approximately 280,000 U.S. troops, and President Nixon sent combat units into Cambodia. However, life went on in the States, and Lorelei and Ted's wedding ceremony took place January 30th, 1970, in

Iowa City at the *Celebration Farm* in the Double Round Barn. Lorelei chose the location, especially for Ted, because of the extraordinary hand-made chandeliers, scent of cedar and artisan wood walls. The organist from their church played Church hymns of Spirit and Love, and Lorelei surprised Ted with a solo: "Whither Thy Goest, I Will Go" from the Book of Ruth. Her strong, soprano voice was like hearing the famous soprano opera singer, Eileen Farrell. Lorelei wore a simple ivory wedding gown with traces of lace around the bodice. Her bouquet was made of Eucalyptus fir and pine decorated with silver stars and balls. Ted wore an ivory wool suit and necktie to match hers. They were a handsome couple, even though the groom looked to be her father's age. Lorelei had decided when she returned from Europe that she would accept her fate and give her life to Ted and the farm. She knew he would give her freedom to research and write, she knew he would never cheat on her, and she knew he was a devout Christian. She also made her final decision that evening, when she saw her nephew waiting up for her in the lobby of the hotel worried about her safety and future. She had wanted to call her father or even her sister, Donna Marie, to help her make the final decision, but she had not needed to call them. She knew that the right thing to do was waiting for her in Iowa. Her father was there to walk her down the aisle, and Lorelei knew that he approved. So, on that destined day, witnessed by family and friends, Lorelei sealed her vows, "from this day forward," with words of commitment at the altar.

The reception was attended by Ted's sole family members: his brother, Otto and his niece, Celia. Celia had been a true friend to Lorelei from the very first time they had met at Church, and was a tremendous blessing for planning her wedding. Lorelei's family was there from Michigan, Georgia and Florida. Hugs, kisses and photos were abounding. The men wore Winter-colored suits, and the ladies wore colorful, Sunday Winter dresses.

It was great seeing David again. Ever since the night she had saved him from the thieves at their hostel, she called him her "God-son." As she hugged him, she whispered into his ear, "Thank you," and he knew she was referring to the secret evening in Italy and waiting up for her in the lobby. David looked older without his European beard and showed off his crew cut to his Aunt. Lorelei hugged her young niece, Viki, who shared her love for family history. Viki was a young teenager growing into a lovely lady with resemblances to her Aunt Lorelei. She hugged her older nephew, Steve, who was a Freshman in college. He was a few inches taller than David, with dark brown hair, but a similar German nose. As she hugged her younger sister, Donna Marie, whom she had always been the closest, tears ran down her eyes. Donna Marie looked into her eyes with her own set of tears and spoke encouraging words: "Lorelei, you will be happy in your new life." Donna Marie had always been "the stronger one" and as lovely as the movie star, Elizabeth Taylor. Lorelei thanked her sister: "You always know what is best for me. Keep me in your prayers."

It had been years since she had seen her much younger siblings, Marty and Donald and was surprised they made it to her wedding. Donald and Marty were in their twenties. Donald looked like the movie-star, Robert Vaughn, and was somewhat of a socialite. Marty was blond, shy and self-conscious of her eyes: one green and one blue. They wore matching pink jumpsuits, which contrasted with the other attendees. Some attendees whispered to each other of the aroma coming from Donald, as he was seen outside smoking funny brown cigarettes. In his top-notch grating voice, he conversed with Marty: "Is it not ironic that a Boston elitist would marry a dirt farmer?" Marty responded in a thick, emotional voice: "I think it is not ironic but very sad. I feel sorry for our sister, as she may not survive such a life." Lorelei overheard their conversation and was about to speak to them harshly, but was rescued by her elderly father, who took her out of the Wedding Barn to comfort her. Her father's soothing voice of reassurance helped her through the reception hours: "Lorelei, this is your second and final marriage. You will resolve to make the best farmer's wife and will remember all that your mother and I taught you and Donna Marie about farming, when you were little girls. Your farm land has the best dark soil, and you will prosper." She hugged her father for his words. Her father started to say something about a new woman he had met, and how he felt guilty because of her mother's unsolved mystery, but was interrupted by a loud noise in the reception room. Lorelei realized that Ted and Otto must have met her brother, Donald. She and her father walked back in and found them arguing about politics. They each had their own version of the turning points for the Vietnam War. Donald's opinion rang out: "It appears that President Nixon is beginning a policy of slow disengagement from the war. However, he has everyone fooled, especially to his own party." Ted questioned him with a cough: "Why do you think he would want to continue this war during his term?" Otto echoed: "What facts do you have that Nixon is fooling the Republicans?" Donald made a prediction, "I tell you this. He cannot be trusted. There will be a political scandal so colossal in his future, that he may be the only president to resign because of misconduct." Lorelei and her father just stood behind the men and allowed them to continue their political discussion. It seemed harmless enough, but Donald was definitely the cynic in the group.

Lorelei had prayed that her Aunt Hope would have been able to come, but she was in a nursing home in Adrian, Michigan. She received an heirloom quilt from her that was made of sheep's wool. From Germany,

Claude and Hanna also sent her a wedding gift of an ancestral photo frame that had belonged to their great grandparents. There was also a beautiful card with a picture of a German farmer and his wife. It was significant to Ted also, because his paternal ancestors were also from Germany. Lorelei was thrilled that they had Germany in common.

It was delightful to see her former students, Lara and Stewart, holding hands and smiling at each other. Lara showed Lorelei her three-stone platinum engagement ring that Stewart had bought in England without her knowledge. They were very happy for Lorelei and her decision, even though they secretly knew how difficult it had been for her. They helped David decorate the "Just Married" sign for the get-away-car, Ted's Old Chevy, and David put cow bells on the bumper.

As the married couple drove off from the reception, Donna Marie painstakingly asked her son, David: "What happened in Europe?

I know my sister. She is keeping something inside." David could see the tears in his mother's eyes of her concern for her sister's decision. David normally would have responded with a joke. But this time, he could not. In his most unusual, serious tone, he said to her: "Mom, please do not ask me. She will never tell any of us, and we will never know what happened." He hesitated, "But, I will tell you now about the night she saved my life." The worried look in his mother's face made him re-consider, because he knew how she worried about him. They were so close, and he had always told her everything. He decided to continue and told her about the two young Italian men who had tried to rob him, and how Lorelei came to his rescue. She frowned: "Why are you now just telling me such a story?" David admitted: "I just did not want to worry you, Mother. Lorelei became my Guardian Angel that evening. I guess I am the son she never had. Is that okay, Mother?" His mother answered in tears: "Of course, it is. She is my beloved sister. I use to share everything with her. I can share you also."

Lorelei and Ted were unable to take a bona-fide honeymoon, because Ted could not leave the farm for more than a day, so he and Lorelei stayed at the Canterbury Inn & Suites in Iowa City. In spite of her accepting foresight, Lorelei was not prepared. Ted was not aware of his strength and had an unusual style of passion. His kisses were rough and mushy. He must have forgotten that he was not on his sheep farm. His amazing energy was like plowing up the pasture, except that his pasture was Lorelei. With inexperience, he was not sure how or when to please his new wife. So, Lorelei gritted her teeth and prayed that she could help him learn how to channel his passion accordingly in the years ahead.

Chapter Seven:

Metamorphosis

In the months that followed, Lorelei gained tremendous admiration for Ted, in spite of their private evenings alone. He was a kind and dependable farmer who worked from sun-up to sun-down with his animals. He maintained fine pastures of hay. He built a conservation pond. He destroyed harmful mole mounds and erosion gullies. He made fences and gates along their land next to the railroad. He inspired their neighbors to improve their land also. He built a modern new garage and continually approved Lorelei's suggestions for renovations inside their home. She gradually encouraged his passion in their private moments with kind words: "Ted, you are such an awesome farmer, and I know you want to shower me with affection as you do your animals! Just take it a little slower with me, and let me show you some affection also. We will pretend we are travelling to different areas on the farm, as we kiss each other. Okay?" Ted's face became blushed and his voice cracked, when he said her nickname: "*Lorei*, I know you probably have more experience in romance than I do, but I really do not want to know about those experiences. But, I will try to be gentler and pleasure you also. Okay?" Lorelei responded with a nickname for him: "Teddy, I know you will try and together we will find more romance than we knew was possible." At least, it was a step in the right direction for the love she needed.

Later that year, Lorelei received an interesting letter from her sister, Donna Marie. She was going to host the German exchange student, Hanna that Lorelei and David had met last Summer! She said that David was of course in his senior year, and that Hanna would also attend his high school. Donna Marie had also received a kind letter from Hanna's father, Claude, who raved about seeing Lorelei last year and asked about her. Lorelei was on the phone immediately to her sister: "I received your letter about Hanna! When will she be staying with you?" Her sister replied, "She is coming at the end of this month and staying for the 2nd semester of school!" Lorelei then asked about Claude, "What did Claude say about me?" Donna Marie replied, "I will send the letter to you. He was so very complimentary. He talked about your discovery that you were distant cousins." Lorelei continued to tell Donna Marie that she was excited for them, and that Hanna would have a wonderful host family. She told her to take pictures and send them, so that she could feel like she was there with them. Donna Marie promised that she would, told her she loved her, and hung up. Lorelei sighed, "Ah me," and had a brief moment of fond memories of Claude.

Being a farmer's wife turned out to be a monumental transition for Lorelei. From Boston Society girl and Ph.D. graduate, Lorelei tried to learn how to raise chickens, sheep, cows and pigs and plant a vegetable garden. At least the renovations of the farmhouse were complete, and Lorelei felt comfortable living in a home that finally had the bathroom and kitchen necessities that she had been accustomed to in Boston. The bedroom antics had not greatly improved, as she had hoped for, but she was at least thankful that most evenings Ted was so exhausted from his farm work, that he slept like a baby as soon as his head hit the pillow.

Their first Christmas together was detailed in her holiday letter to her sister. As Donna Marie read it, she had to quickly get to the end of the letter to make sure her sister had survived. It read, "Ted told me when we were dating that he hardly ever had time to celebrate or decorate for the holidays, because there was so much work to do on the farm at that time. Even with the part-time farm-hands he hired, he always allowed them time off for Christmas Eve and Christmas Day, so he was usually the only worker, but now he had my help! Well, it was Christmas Eve, and I called Ted to the supper table, as the sun was going down. I had been beside him all day helping with the chores, except when I worked in the barn alone, and then took time to make a pork chop casserole for supper. So, when he came in to eat, we sat down together to rest and discuss what would need to be done the next day. Ted was always polite about my cooking, even though I know his first wife cooked better, because comments would slip out about how she had cooked the same meal, and it tasted differently. We were finishing our casserole, and I took the plates to the sink under the window overlooking the barn. And that is when I saw it! The barn was on fire! I yelled to Ted, and he and I ran quickly out to investigate. The fire was just inside the barn, but Ted told me to call the fire station anyway! We both knew that the fire station was not close by and would take about 30 minutes, so by that time, Ted could hopefully extinguish it himself. Donna Marie, he was so brave! He knew exactly the right steps to take. He took out the animals first, he gave me orders firm but not in panic, as if he was in control of the entire situation. He was. He was able to put out the fire using blankets and several fire extinguishers. We were not sure what had caused it. Neither of us smoked, so it could not have been from a cigarette. We had a kerosene heater that I could have forgotten to turn off in my haste to cook supper, and I told Ted about it, but he was very protective of my feelings at that time. He told me that it did not matter how the fire was started. It was over. The only damage was one of the stalls would have to be rebuilt. I was able to cancel the fire truck en route by calling them directly and telling them that my husband had successfully put out the fire. I was so proud of him! The next day, I helped him rebuild the stall. We were like two newlyweds with the same mission. We enjoyed Christmas morning, not sharing store-bought gifts, but just sharing coffee with each other and looking into the fireplace of how thankful we were that the barn had not burned to the ground. We read together and prayed together. Merry Christmas to you, my sweet sister. All is well in Iowa. *Love you Always, Lorelei*."

The Sunday before Thanksgiving the next year, in 1972, Ted and Lorelei were sitting in the back pews of their Church, because Lorelei had a bad cough and did not want to disturb anyone. Several of the farm families were not in attendance due to the cold weather and chores, so the Church had only about 20 people in attendance. The ushers usually were at the back during the service in case someone else came in, but on this particular Sunday, there was only one usher available, and as he was an older man, he sat down two pews ahead of Ted and

Lorelei, instead of standing by the door. During the first hymn, a middle-aged white man walked in. He was dressed in dust-covered rag clothes, hung his head down revealing his pre-mature gray-matted hair and wore sandals on his dirty feet. At first, Lorelei thought it might be a surprise presentation for the upcoming Advent Season, and that the man was just an actor. However, Ted read her mind and poked her to be on the alert. The grungy, bad-smelling, poor homeless man sat down right beside them on the same pew. He did not say a word during the entire service, and he did not bother anyone. Out of the corner of their eyes, Ted and Lorelei both saw him praying silently to himself. Lorelei quietly pulled out a piece of scratch paper before the service was over, and she wrote a note to her husband, "Ted, do you think we should take this man home with us and feed him?" She slipped it to him, and as he read it, he looked at his wife and nodded, as if to say, "Yes, it would be the right thing to do." So, when the service was over, and before the man got up to leave, Ted who was sitting closest to him, caught him gently by the arm and asked: "Sir, would you like to come home with us and have a home-cooked meal?" You could see that the man's eyes began to tear, as he responded in a choked voice: "Oh, yes, thank you." They escorted him out of the church, not bothering to say anything to anyone or making a big deal about it, but walked him to their car and helped him into the back seat. When they arrived home, Lorelei immediately offered him soup and sandwiches and sweet tea. They discovered his name was Allen, and that he was a Vietnam Veteran. He had a daughter who received an art scholarship and was studying in Europe. He could not find employment, so something told him to walk into that Church and pray. His prayer was answered by Ted and Lorelei. He stayed with them through Thanksgiving, cleaned up and shaved and borrowed some of Ted's clothes. He woke up at the crack of dawn and helped Ted with the chores on the farm, relieving Lorelei for household work. It was a special Thanksgiving for all of them. Lorelei and Ted helped Allen regain his strength, spiritually and physically, and, he in turn, gave them the peace of mind that they had been useful to someone who needed their help. Allen was a carpenter by trade, and Ted was able to give him the name of a company that could possibly hire him. He wrote to his daughter, who was scheduled to be in England for Christmas, and he knew that he would be able to live with her when she returned in the New Year. They told Allen he could stay until then, but he insisted that he would stay in the local motel in town, until he was hired. They paid him for helping with the chores and an extra two hundred to help him with living expenses in December. When he left the day after Thanksgiving, he told them that someday he would be back to repay them for their kindness.

By 1974, Lorelei's metamorphosis was complete. She was a full-fledged farmer's wife and suffered with Ted the challenges that affronted them. U.S. farm income decreased about $5 billion dollars, and some farmers went bankrupt. Ted and Lorelei would not have survived without their savings. The feed grain supply was the lowest since 1957, with warmer than average and cooler than average, inconsistent weather conditions. Lorelei had to console Ted on several occasions, as he would cry out to her in his weakest voice: "What are we going to do if our savings is depleted?" Lorelei would respond: "We will be okay. I will start writing for profit and teach additional evening classes at Iowa Wesleyan."

Several days after that conversation, Ted developed pneumonia. He was sneezing constantly, hacking and coughing and worse, he had a very high fever. Lorelei tried all of the remedies she knew her mother had tried when she was a little girl.

She also called the Church practitioner, who came to their home for several hours, read and prayed with them. However, for three days, Ted's fever did not subside. On the third day, as she sat by his side, Lorelei remembered the 1894 Kate Chopin short story, <u>The Story of an Hour</u>. It was a story of a young woman, with a weak heart, who found out within the setting of an hour, that her husband had been killed in a railroad accident; all evidence pointed to the fact that he was not one of the survivors. So, in mourning, during that same hour, she could not help herself. She thought of her freedom from the bondage of marriage. She started planning, where she would travel, and how she would finally be able to achieve her dreams. Ironically, her husband was a survivor after all and came in the front door of their home. In double-irony, she was the one who fell dead to the floor, when she saw her husband alive. Lorelei compared the short story to her own life. What if Ted passed away? What would she do with the farm? Would she be able to travel abroad again? Would she be able to achieve the dreams she had possibly sacrificed? She remembered she had lived alone for almost ten years after her divorce with Fred.

Her thoughts were deadened, as Ted's fever broke within the hour. She felt so guilty for thinking of that short story and only of herself.

Before the economic downfall, Lorelei had ordered a special loom from Finland that she had seen on her first tour of Europe. She remembered that the loom was unique for the process of warping. Ted had even suggested she try weaving as a hobby that would help her unwind in the cold Winter evenings. Ted also finished making the cupboard-shelf-fan-holding arrangement over the former breakfast bar that used to separate the living room and the former kitchen. Lorelei stained everything a rich, mahogany color. With the Finland loom, as her motivator, Lorelei's projects included weaving, painting and remodeling the guest bedroom in preparation for her writing and research. A mutual family research buff from Church gave her a gift: a beautiful, pinewood cabinet, the size of a china cabinet, so that she could organize her ancestor notebooks and census record files.

Ted also completed a gate between the hall and living room, so that their dog, Bernard, could get into the living room when he was in the house on cold days. When he was a puppy, he chewed up everything that he could. Ted told Lorelei the humorous puppy story: "Once he got hold of a throw rug and tugged on both ends until he ripped it in two. I heard him in the other room but did not investigate in time. You should have seen the remains of that rug!" Lorelei laughed visualizing the scenario. The farm animals were their common ground. They both loved all the animals, from the dogs to the cats to the chickens to the sheep to the cows. Lorelei tried to make up a name for each and every animal. She even named one of the bulls, Humbert.

One particular evening, she and Ted discussed the names that Lorelei had given to the new litter of kittens. Ted asked her: "Why did you name two of the kittens, Harlequin and Columbine? Where did you get those names?" Lorelei explained that she named them after the Italian Comedy performers of comic male and female clowns: *Commedia dell'arte*. It caught her by surprise that Ted had reminded her of Italy by asking questions. She brushed it off: "Oh, you know I love anything and everything about the theatre, and the kittens just reminded me of the silly clowns." She changed the subject by telling him that she named the black kitten after the famous horse, Beauty. She told him of the "Black Beauty" movie with her favorite actress, Elizabeth Taylor, who always reminded her of Donna Marie. Ted shifted his thoughts to her sister resembling the actress and did not approach the subject of Italy again.

However, Ted saw something in Lorelei's eyes that disturbed him, as she had described the clowns of the Italian Theatre.

At the Thanksgiving holiday in 1974, Lorelei and Ted had a surprise visit from her God-son, David, and his fiancée, Eileen. Eileen was a farmer's daughter from Mableton, Georgia and had known David's deceased father, who had also been a farmer in Tennessee. They were both wearing their casual, long sleeve, ranch-hand overalls and were ready to visit the farm. Eileen had long, silky blond hair and blue eyes that accentuated her smile. She was just the right height to match David, and his red hair and rosy cheekbones blended with her dimples.

It seemed that a seed of thought was planted during their visit, and a serious discussion followed for Lorelei and Ted. Eileen was delighted by all of the farm animals, especially the sheep. She was a natural with them, as the animals could always sense an animal lover, and David shared her enthusiasm. Lorelei could tell they were in love. They were always laughing and kissing. Eileen showed her expertise in everything, from electrical lighting and modern designs to solutions in handling weeds in the garden. She told Ted all about her father's bale farm, their grass mixes and horse alfalfa, but about twenty years ago she said her father also raised milking cows. They currently had only a hundred acres, because during the Depression, her father had to sell some of his land, and it broke his heart. Her brother in Mableton had recently taken over the farm.

On Thanksgiving Day, David and Eileen continued to show their aptitude to farm living. They both knew how to shell peas and cook. David made a special compliment to his aunt: "There is nothing in this world that tastes better than your country fried corn, right from the garden! We came all this way so that my fiancé could experience for herself the special flavor of Iowa corn!" They all laughed at his exaggerated reason for coming to Iowa. Ted and Lorelei felt like they were eating the festive meal with their own children. Eileen helped cook the turkey and dressing, David stuffed it, Lorelei made all the vegetables into casseroles, and Ted sat at the head of the table, praying a Thanksgiving prayer for their visit. It was a memorable event.

Before they left in their green Dodge rental, Lorelei whispered in their ears: "You could not possibly know what this visit meant to Ted and me. I know this may sound crazy, but after your studying Agriculture in college, David, and Eileen, after you have finished Seminary school, would you please come visit us again and stay for a longer visit?" It seemed she was hinting at something, but David and Eileen did not want to pry, so Eileen answered in her thick Southern accent: "We would be honored to visit you again and stay longer." They hugged Ted, which was also very unusual, because he never hugged anyone except his niece. Lorelei kissed them both on their cheeks. They waved goodbye.

The important discussion that followed David and Eileen's visit was about an heir. Lorelei and Ted worried about Ted's farm that had been in the family since 1850. Since he had no children, she had no children, and his only niece had no children, they did not know who would be their heir. Lorelei posed the question: "Ted, will your family farm be sold off to the State of Iowa, if we die without an heir?" Ted bleakly answered: "Yes, I am afraid that might happen. As you know, my brother has no other children except Celia, who has no children, but I think he has a very close friend, who may be his heir. You and I need to make a decision, in case something happens to either one of us, or both of us. I will make an appointment with our attorney, and we will draw up the papers to reflect our decision. Okay?" Lorelei nodded in agreement. It also gave her an idea. She ran to the attic to get her collection of European coins that she kept in a metal lock box. She came back downstairs and told Ted she wanted to bury the box, as a treasure chest, for the future heir. She would create a graphic map and enclose it with their Will. Ted asked her: "How many coins do you have in there?" She had never shown them to him, so she took time to explain each one of her treasured coins from Italy, France, Germany, England, Spain, China, Japan, Hong Kong, Switzerland, Austria, Scotland, The Netherlands, Monaco, Greece, Portugal, Egypt, India and the Philippines. She also showed him the silver dollars she had saved from her childhood. She explained: "The total value of everything in the chest is approximately a thousand dollars in today's value, but just think what these coins could be worth for our heir in the future? I feel excited knowing that we can provide an emergency fund also!" Ted was amazed at her generosity and imagination for a treasure hunt. So, together, she and Ted went outside into the pasture and found a spot underneath a huge oak tree. With his shovel, he dug a very deep hole and helped his wife place the box into the hole and covered it with black dirt and leaves. It was like burying a time capsule. She was satisfied.

By Christmas of 1974, they had a dozen new hens that kept their rooster and two ducks company. Although Ted did not have the funds to give gifts for Christmas that year and was unable to hire farm-hands, he did enjoy watching a few of the classics on television with Lorelei in the evenings. They especially enjoyed the 1970 Classic Musical Movie, Charles Dickens' *A Christmas Carol* with Albert Finney, as Scrooge.

Their daily lives revolved around their animals. The new hens were laying eggs like mad. They had eggs in everything: custards, cakes, eggs to feed the dogs and cats, and still there were too many, so Lorelei started giving them to friends at her college, and her friends offered to purchase them from her, but she always refused to take any money from them.

Ted always encouraged Lorelei to attend the theatre without him. She would offer to stay home to help him with the chores, but especially during that Christmas month, he told her he would be able to manage without her. He felt he had deprived her in the previous Christmas seasons of special performances she loved. So, Lorelei was able to attend the Christmas Convocation's comic version of *How the Grinch Stole Christmas*. Members from the Iowa and the Midwest Arts Councils shared with her the possibilities of sponsoring an Art Train. They told her the train would go throughout the U.S. with American paintings from all over the country, worth millions of dollars. They hoped Creston would be one of the six stops the train would make in Iowa. It was exciting to Lorelei to feel a part of the world she was accustomed to again. She also found everyone hopeful that the Guthrie Theatre, the regional professional theatre based in Minneapolis and internationally acclaimed, would be coming to Creston to present *The Summoning of Everyman,* a late 15th century English morality play. They were in the process of signing a contract and starting the publicity. If it materialized, she would definitely be present at that play!

Lorelei also attended the Arts Festival at the Creston College where she had taught part-time. There was Christmas music by the Music Department, and then the Art Department had refreshments and exhibits. At the Reader's Theatre, she also enjoyed the performance from her former peers of Dylan Thomas' *Under Milk Wood,* about an omniscient narrator who invites the audience to listen to the dreams and innermost thoughts of the inhabitants of a fictional small Welsh fishing village. Lorelei enjoyed the performance immensely.

When she arrived home that Christmas Eve, she was surprised to see a black Ford Truck in the driveway near the farmhouse. She quickly ran in to see who would be visiting that late in the evening. She walked in and heard laughter. At the table enjoying a huge turkey dinner with all the trimmings, was Allen, the man they had helped several years ago. With him was a young woman, who he introduced heartily: "Lorelei, this is my lovely daughter, Jessica. We hope that you do not mind that we stopped by. Ever since you both helped me, I told Jessica I would love to pay you back. We have brought you a turkey dinner to share our blessings with you!" Lorelei clapped in excitement, "Of course, we are so happy to see you! You look so well! Jessica, it is so nice to meet you! Please tell us all about your success! Jessica, I would love to hear about your travels in Europe! So, she sat down, grabbed a plate, and the conversation went from his carpentry job, to his daughter's successful art career. She was moving to Chicago to open her own art studio! Jessica shared some of the highlights of her studies in Europe. She and Lorelei were able to discuss their favorite art museums. Allen also handed Ted an envelope with the money he owed them, but

Ted gave it back to him and said, "Think of it as a gift from friends." They shared a good evening and promised to keep in touch.

Two years later, Lorelei attended David's college graduation and wedding. It was a small wedding ceremony in Mableton. Although, Ted did not attend, he made sure that Lorelei gave his blessings to the happy couple, and the wedding gift was a special, wood-carving set that Ted made in his tool shed. Lorelei was so proud of her God-son's graduation with a Bachelor of Science in Agriculture. Eileen was in her final year of Seminary and would soon be a Minister of Religion. She was also able to reunite with her sister, niece and nephew, and his wife and high school sweetheart, Patricia. It was her first time meeting Patricia, and she gave her a special compliment on how pretty she was: "Steve, your wife resembles Jacqueline Kennedy, with her smooth skin and kind eyes." Patricia blushed and thanked her. Lorelei also apologized for not attending their wedding: "I am so sorry I missed your wedding last year, but I was just unable to leave the farm!" Patricia responded, "We understood. Thank you again for the special bride and groom porcelain figurines!" Steve told his aunt he was still attending college for Business Management, and Patricia would soon be a Licensed Christian Counselor. Lorelei was very impressed of their chosen careers.

A week after David's wedding, Lorelei attended Lara and Stewart's back in Des Moines, Iowa. Their wedding was a small wedding as David's had been, as Lara had just graduated from Principia College in Illinois, and Stewart, from Frank Lloyd Wright's School of Architecture in Arizona. Lorelei and Ted's wedding gift was a porcelain tea set, and David and Eileen's was a wedding gift basket of chocolates. They were still on their honeymoon, so were unable to attend, but had given Lorelei their gift to take personally to them. Even though Eileen had not met Lara and

Stewart, she felt close to them from their many letters to David.

One morning in 1976, as Lorelei was directing the dress-rehearsal for her students of "The 60's" dramatic play for that evening, she was summoned to the school office for a phone call. It was from Elaine, her half-sister telling her that their father had just passed away. Elaine learned from her mother, his new wife, that he had a sudden heart attack at the breakfast table. She called for an ambulance, but he passed within moments, and when it arrived, they could not revive him. Lorelei knew she would need to attend the funeral services, but she was also needed at the play that evening. One of her honor students, Cody, had written the play especially for Lorelei, as he knew she would support his efforts to become a dramatic writer. It was a drama about a family moving to a new school, and Cody choreographed it and helped Lorelei as director. So, instead of postponing the play for her father's funeral, Lorelei felt that

Cody would be able to take over as director. She attended her father's funeral in Florida, was gone for three days and found out that the play had been such a huge success that another college in the area asked them to perform, so Lorelei was back in time to see them perform after all. She was so proud of her students and of her faith in Cody.

One day after class, not long after Cody's grand performance, another student walked into the classroom and asked if he could speak with her for a moment. Lorelei noticed that he had a tablet in his hand, so she speculated that he wanted to ask her questions about the writing project due by the end of the week. His name was Deanie, and he did have questions about the project, but then his young voice changed into something else. He pulled out a folded letter to read to her in a sexy tone: "You are my favorite teacher ever! You are the most beautiful woman I have ever known! You have been so kind to me and have encouraged me to write. You have helped me more than you'll ever know. I love you, Miss Lorelei. Will you let me hug you?" Lorelei was taken aback. She had students praise her before, but nothing to that extent, and she knew he was not a student with a mental challenge. She was leery. She gave him a quick hug and responded cautiously: "Deanie, you are a very talented, young man. Continue your writing in confidence. However, you must not be disillusioned by me, or any of your other teachers. You have to keep your relationship with an adult strictly professional, in your college studies and in the workplace. Do you understand?" Very saddened, he nodded, put the love letter back in his pocket and walked out of the classroom. Lorelei was concerned she had hurt his feelings, but she had to say those words to him to let him know the love letter was inappropriate. From that time forward, Deanie was shy and quiet in class and never approached her again.

Lorelei became a writer from her farm experiences for Mt. Pleasant's, *The News*, in which she titled her weekly submissions: "Out on the Farm." It was an outlet for her to write, as she worked the farm. She was able to inspire her readers to share the awakened pleasures of owning land and a farm. She provided details of raising sheep from reproduction, health, lambing, feeding and predators, to shearing, marketing and gardening.

In 1977, she wrote about the chickens and hens: "Indeed, if someone had told me a few years ago that, mostly for the fun of it, I would be raising a few chickens, I would not have believed it. But here I am, doing just that. The pleasures are many. It gives satisfaction, to see the scrawny sales barn hens we picked up for 30 cents each become fine, producing hens."

That same year, she wrote about their cats: "I have heard of farms with as many as thirty cats. Whether one has one or thirty, however, he [she] cannot help appreciating them. They are a valuable part of the farmer's rodent-control program." Lorelei often had to remind

Ted about their value, especially when Heidi, one of Lorelei's favorite cats, but not Ted's, would hide in the evenings after supper and sneak inside through the upstairs window to annoy him. He would yell for Lorelei to put her back outside.

She also wrote about the snakes: "The non-venomous, Iowan milk snake was very secretive, so I only saw him once. Ah, but his colors were phenomenal! He had a brown ground color and rusty red body blotches, similar to a fox snake. He looked to be about 52 inches in length. He only let me view him for a moment, and then slithered on his way."

Lorelei tried to share her New England experiences in her articles: "I've had vegetable gardens in New England and elsewhere, and weeds in New England were never much of a problem. The soil was often rocky and less rich, and somehow the varieties of non-wanted plants were never as vigorous or big or persistent." She compared her vegetable garden in Iowa to her gardens in Boston. She wrote: "Here on the [Iowa] farm, however, we have not only rich soil but bigger gardens. We can even use machinery (and we do) for plowing and planting the sweet corn."

Lorelei provided solutions in her articles for the weeds. She suggested herbicide and urged the consistency of hoeing. She wrote about mulching materials that were helpful. She stated that healthy plants shaded the ground against weeds and required feeding, watering, thinning out and transplanting stragglers. Lorelei also shared her new ideas for an exotic touch to one's garden: "leeks, marble ball celeriac, American purple top rutabagas, kale, early white Vienna Kohl Rabi and mammoth Sandwich Island salsify."

Lorelei also read every book she could find from the large homesteading collection at the Iowa City Public Library. However, she learned the most from watching Ted on a daily basis. He was a natural, as his father before him, Henry, of German descent, who had settled in Iowa in the mid-1800's. One excerpt submitted in September, from Lorelei's writings was about their brown hen: "The brown hen was persistent. She wanted to raise her own chicks. Others might sit on an available pile of eggs for an hour or so, but then they would be distracted or bored, or they would be forced off by another hen who wanted the place. But our brown hen had a mission." Lorelei had a mission also. She was determined to beat the odds of her insipid situation on the farm.

She usually concluded her articles with a bit of whimsical humor: "Ah, yes, there is nothing quite as fine as being able to bring back a dishpan full of lettuce or peas or soup greens or rhubarb or strawberries or corn or tomatoes or ... well, the list is as long as the summer. Weeds? Who said they were a problem? Nonsense!"

She wrote to her sister about their lambs and sheep: "Ted got two more sheep yesterday, to bring our total up to thirty lambs and sheep. We have mostly lambs on one side of a large shed and mostly sheep on the other, with a fence between. The lambs can get out into a yard where I feed them grain three times a day and water them, while the sheep have their own pasture and watering trough. Now that the pasture is getting quite tall from our recent rains, one can hardly see the sheep when they are out grazing. Our garden is plentiful with lots of lettuce, radishes, strawberries, raspberries and tomatoes. Ah, the life of a farmer's wife giving you my monthly report! *Always, Lorelei.*"

She was also able to visit the Genealogical Collections in both the Iowa Library and the Latter Day Saints' local Family History Center. Her mother had never known who her father was, so that was one brick wall that Lorelei wanted to jump over. It happened one day at the Family History Center, that she was able to locate the marriage certificate for her mother's parents. With the marriage certificate, Lorelei had finally come across the name of her mother's father. "Could that help her find her mother?" she wondered.

In the late summer of 1977, Donna Marie and Viki visited Lorelei and Ted on their farm. Lorelei told them she had visions of more ideas for the upstairs' attic and loft. She wanted to include a spare bedroom in the loft for visitors, such as Viki and her brothers. David and Steve were unable to visit at that time, so Viki took pictures of the sheep and other farm animals to share with them when they returned home. On their second day of touring the farm and its 200 acres, Lorelei realized that Ted's favorite dog, Bernard, the beagle, which was also her favorite, since she had grown to love him, was missing. She called for him and walked to the other side of the pasture to see if he was with Ted. Ted told her he had not seen him since daybreak. Lorelei asked her sister to go with her to find him and asked Viki to stay behind at the farm in case he showed up. So, they walked the entire distance from north to south on the farm road, about two miles, and Lorelei knocked on every neighbor's door asking if they had seen him. Donna Marie was amazed at how much she loved that animal to take such time and effort to find him. Finally, they arrived back at the farm just before sundown. Viki stood at the front door, and there beside her was Bernard and a friend. Viki explained: "About fifteen minutes ago, I was at watch at the front window, and I saw Bernard and a female beagle, both nudging their heads together, prancing to the barn. They stayed in the barn, until about five minutes ago when they came up to the front, looking for food." Lorelei and Donna Marie looked at each other, and then at Bernard and his new companion, and they just laughed! Lorelei gave Bernard a gentle scolding. She knew the female probably belonged to someone down the road, so she said she would wait until Ted came in for supper to discuss with him. Bernard and the female were fed and watered, and Lorelei, Donna Marie and Viki went in to prepare supper.

Before the final day of their visit, Lorelei showed her sister and niece her favorite spot on the farm. She would go there on days that troubled her, where she needed to meditate and pray. It helped her re-analyze her situation and be thankful for it. It was a peaceful spot, far away from the farmhouse, from the barn, from the chores. It was still on their 200 acres, but it was near the flowing river where the turquoise water reminded her of the Mediterranean Sea. There was a huge rock similar to *Her Rock* on the Rhine near the water's edge, high enough to see for miles around. Donna Marie, Viki and Lorelei sat together on *Lorelei's U.S. Rock* and held each other's hands in silence. Each had a heartbreak to think about. Donna Marie had loved a man with such passion and sacrifice that when he died, it took something out of her that she could never recover. Viki thought about her high school sweetheart, and how he had broken her heart and moved to Arizona their junior year. Lorelei, of course, was thinking about Humberto, and what might have been. They also gave a group prayer for their mother that wherever she was, they prayed she was well and happy.

Lorelei updated Viki on her recent research discovery about their maternal grandparents and showed her the ancestry pinewood cabinet. Viki was in her passion zone, as her aunt showed her the legacy of information. She asked: "How can I help you? How many generations have you gone back?" So, her aunt was able to give her details and instructions on how she could help. She was comforted, knowing that all of her hard work and research would go to her niece.

Viki and Donna Marie's visit was over too soon. They shook hands with Ted and thanked him for the visit, and then hugged Lorelei, knowing it might be a long time before they saw each other again.

In January of 1980, Lorelei and Ted celebrated their tenth wedding anniversary. Most of those years had been spent learning from Ted by watching him. He was very patient with her in regards to anything that had to do with the farm work. They shared anniversary gifts. Lorelei gave Ted a new pocket watch, because his had been broken when he dropped it at Church one Sunday. Ted gave Lorelei a dozen red roses and a beautiful card with a picture of an Iowa farm. Lorelei sincerely told him: "I love you." In return, Ted replied, "I love you more than you will ever know." They kissed as ten years of kissing before, and although it had not been the romantic ride that Lorelei would have envisioned, it was the life she had chosen, and she was content enough.

At Christmas in 1980, Lorelei and Ted made some changes, and the animals were especially cooperative. They took the rams out from among the ewes and put them in a stall by themselves. They put rings in the pigs' noses and put them in with the steers. They had to have rings in their noses so they would not root up all the dirt and make holes under the fences so they and the steers could get out. But they loved their new freedom there. Lorelei and Ted brought a creep gate over from one barn to the other so the young lambs could have a special place to "creep" through that the older sheep could squeeze through, in order to get extra feed that way. One of Ted's Christmas gifts to Lorelei was her very own white-faced ewe that she named Christie-Lee.

Lorelei also started another term as the First Reader in their Church. A lovely girl who just graduated from Iowa Wesleyan would substitute for Lorelei as soloist from time to time. Lorelei even bought a new dress for her first appearance as reader. She found a white, velvet dress at a discount store, and took it home, trimmed the sleeves with fur trim that she had in her trim box and made a couple other alterations. Lorelei also learned how to spin wool from their ewes, so she made a lovely, white, wool sweater to match. It came as a surprise to Lorelei, when Ted gave her a long-overdue compliment, when she wore her new outfit to Church.

At the beginning of 1981, Lorelei was out feeding the young ewes, when she heard Ted calling her name: "Lorei, honey, you have a phone call from Adrian." Lorelei knew it must be about her Aunt Hope. The woman over the phone was from the nursing home in Adrian, and told her that her aunt had just passed away that morning. Lorelei told Ted the news and made plans to drive to Michigan the next day. Lorelei was the only relative able to attend her funeral. Her sister, Donna Marie, and her other siblings could not make the trip at that time. Her Aunt Hope was honored with a Memorial Hall named after her at Adrian College for her dedicated, 40 years as Language Professor. Lorelei spoke from the local Adrian radio station praising her Aunt Hope's accomplishments, including the fact that she was the Founder of the local Humane Society.

In 1981, their lambing was over, with the last of their young yearling ewes having a lamb. Both barns were full of lambs of all sizes and shapes. They used two different types of rams to breed them with, and the ewes were several other breeds, so it was an interesting and motley mixture. Lorelei took lots of notes about raising sheep, because one of the books she was working on was titled "Adventures of an Amateur Iowa Shepherd," which would be about her experiences raising sheep. It really was a fun and interesting activity, and it brought in enough dribbles of money so that she could afford to keep writing until it yielded money. She told Ted one day, "The wonderful thing about raising sheep is (besides the fact that they grow on you, and you become very fond of them) is that they are a small enough livestock so that a woman can manage with them, and if one raises enough of them, they bring in a nice income." Ted nodded and agreed with her and hoped she was correct.

In June of 1981, Lorelei had an unexpected request from her niece. She phoned to make sure she could visit before she bought her airline ticket. Lorelei knew she was off for the summer from her high school teaching, so maybe she just needed a holiday before going back in August. She told Viki that she would pick her up at the airport, once she knew the time schedule. She arrived a week later, in the late afternoon. Her aunt was waiting for her with open arms! Viki ran into her aunt's embrace, and they both hugged in kindred spirit. They were so much alike, in appearance, in careers, in passion for genealogy research and travelling, and Lorelei would soon find out the real reason Viki was there for a visit.

As they walked in the door to the farm, Viki greeted Ted with a short hug, and Ted motioned for them to sit down to supper. To Lorelei's surprise, he had laid out nice dinnerware for Viki and had finished cooking the roast that Lorelei had put in the oven earlier. They had fresh vegetables and fruits from the garden, and Viki again was overwhelmed with joy at the delicious taste of the farm food! After supper, they chatted for a little while, but could tell that Viki needed to turn in early, so Lorelei showed her the small guest room and bath, and Viki said, "Thank you. We will talk in the morning, okay?" Her aunt kissed her gently on the forehead and said goodnight.

The next morning, Viki rose early to help her aunt in the kitchen for breakfast. She knew Lorelei had chores to do also on the farm, so she offered to help her with those also, and then they could talk. First, she wanted to see the sheep again and the other farm animals. So, they ate breakfast alone, as Ted had already had his coffee and was out on the far end trying to repair one of his tractors. Viki was so thrilled to see the sheep! Her Aunt introduced her to Christie-Lee, the white-faced ewe that Ted had given her for Christmas in 1980. She saw the beagle, Bernard again, and met the cats,

Harlequin and Columbine, and Lorelei explained the origins of their names. At about ten o'clock, Lorelei and Viki were finally able to go into the farmhouse and have their serious conversation. They sat down across from each other on the sofas. Viki began in a very southern, somber tone: "Aunt Lorelei, I am in a pickle. I have spoken with my mother and oldest brother, Steve, and asked their advice, but somehow I feel that you have the most wisdom. From your detailed letters throughout the years, my mother and I both agree that you have the most experience in choosing love and romance. You had a wonderful Bostonian husband, whom you loved very much. You went to Europe three times and had wonderful opportunities to meet kind, romantic Italian and German gentlemen. You now have a devoted farmer who loves you very much. Am I correct so far?" Lorelei smiled her devious smile, "Yes, you have the basics. I will let you tell me your dilemma first, and then maybe I can fill in the missing pieces."

Viki's story had so many similar conceptuals to her Aunt Lorelei's, that it was difficult for her to sit still and not interrupt. Viki continued in a low voice, but also remembered that her Aunt could only hear out of her right ear, so she leaned that way: "I know I am young, but I have already had three proposals. I want to make sure I make the right choice. I also may be a little silly about analyzing my kisses, but a kiss to me says so much about that person. Do you agree, aunt?" She gave me a very big smile and nodded. "Well, my first proposal was last year from a man that my mother introduced to me from her office. He was a fairly decent, nice, red-haired man, but such a country boy and had no ambitions or goals for his future. His kisses were rather rough and sloppy. When he asked me to marry him after only six months of dating, I postponed my answer to him, thinking that this was the first man who had ever proposed to me, so I should not give a hasty answer. Then I met another man, quiet older than me, whom my brother Steve introduced. We played tennis together, and we dated for about four months. I found out that he cared more about watching television than paying any attention to me. He watched any and all sports and was glued to the television. His kisses were much better, because they were quick. I guess he needed to get back to the television. However, he must have thought that I cared for him, and he for me, for he proposed during the holidays. I told him we needed to date other people first, so I left him hanging. Then, my best friend gave me the address of my dashing, high school sweetheart, who was in an Arizona prison for something he didn't do. Immediately, I felt sorry for him, after she told me all the facts. I started writing him, and we sent many cassette tapes with our voices, back and forth, for several months like a courtship. I even travelled to Arizona to visit him one weekend and stayed with his mother. His kisses were as I remembered them in high school, experimental and passionate. He talked about marriage when his appeal was won. I told him I would wait for him. I had not intended on dating anyone else, with three men dangling, but then I met Albert at a Church activity. I noticed him right away, his kind face and down-to-earth shuffle through the hall, even before we all went out to the pizza place, as a group. When we went in our separate cars, I walked up to the restaurant door by myself and right behind me was Albert, opening the door for me! His jacket sleeve brushed my shoulder, and I felt thrilled! He looked into my eyes, and then I knew. It was a sign of fate! Our first kiss was soothing and magical. He is so smart and funny, and such a gentleman and was born in Alabama. We discovered the amazing coincidence that we had grown up in the same neighborhood and probably had eaten at the same *Mister Donut* in Smyrna! He and his sister had attended the same high school as my brothers, just a few years behind them! Oh, and I found out that his mother and father had passed away when he and his sister were very young, so they were raised by aunts and uncles. They had lived in Alabama, New York, Arizona and Georgia! He and I had so much in common with our travels! He is four years older than me. He has recently asked me about our future. He wants to know how I feel about marriage. I told him I would let him know after my visit with you! What do you think? What if I make the wrong decision, and I choose the wrong man? Do I base my decision on kisses? Can you sort this out for me?"

Viki looked into her aunt's emerald eyes that twinkled like the middle-aged, Mrs. Claus, and she saw the answer, but wanted to hear it from her aunt: "My sweet niece, I can see that you saw the answer in my eyes. But I will give you a brief summary of my experiences, so that you can understand your choice. Yes, I loved Fred very much, but as you know he found another, and someday I must see him again with his new wife and see that they are happy to forgive him in my heart. But I had complete confidence that I would love again, as I had with Fred. I found love more intense than Fred's with an Italian gentleman, that I met when your brother was with me in Europe. I also met a German cousin, who also confessed his love to me, but I realized that my love for him was the family connection. I then knew at that time, that I had a very important decision to make. Would I stay in Europe for the Italian, or perhaps even for the German gentleman? Or, would I come back to Iowa and marry a man, who was devoted, faithful and fatefully meant to be my husband? I chose Ted. Do I love him? Yes, I do. I learned there are two types of love. There is the passionate, earth-shaking type that thrills our inner soul, but can have unknown side-effects, and then there is the steadfast, secure, peaceful love that does not. Do you understand what I mean when I say side-effects?" Viki answered, "Yes, I think you mean possible infidelity effects?" Lorelei nodded sadly, "Yes, if your man is too handsome, it is possible he might find another." Lorelei cleared her throat and concluded, "So, Viki, I think we both know your chosen one. Perhaps, you have a little bit of both loves for him? Not only did you say you met him at Church, as I did Ted, but you know without a doubt in your mind and heart, that he will never forsake you." Viki reached out with tears in her eyes to hug her Aunt Lorelei, who had just given the key to her heart. She could go back with confidence that she was making the right choice. Her aunt quickly ran out of the room and came back with a small, black velvet case. She explained: "Viki, inside this case is the wedding ring that Fred bought me many years ago. Your Albert may want to buy you his own personal ring. Either way, you can save this ring for your daughter someday. It is a valuable heirloom." Lorelei opened the box and inside was a Tiffany's ring in platinum, with rose-cut and round brilliant diamonds set in cobblestones. Viki's mouth dropped in amazement: "Oh, Lorelei, how stunning and unique! I will be honored to either wear it or save it for my daughter! Thank you so much for thinking of me!"

By the Autumn of 1981, another ewe had twins, so they were doing a bit of Fall lambing, though not on the scale of their Spring lambing. Their geese had grown to full size and were very friendly and noisy and followed them around. Their beagle, Bernard was still eager to learn how to isolate the sheep, but he tried to nip them on the side. Ted finished his corn picking and as a tradition, he prepared oyster stew to celebrate getting the corn picked. When the ground was still too wet from the rains to pick corn, they went up to Kalona for a sale at the sales barn to take one of their rams to sell and buy a Billy goat. It was quite an experience, for Kalona was Mennonite country, and a whole parking lot at the sales barn was ringed by a railing, where the Mennonites could tie up their horses and black carriages, bearing red triangular slow-moving vehicle emblems on the back. It was like a relic of the past, as the railing all around the edge were filled with horses and carriages, maybe fifty or more. Ted bought his Billy goat, a fine black one who evidently had belonged to a Mennonite family, for on the way home, as they drove through the streets of Kalona, they met one of their horses and carriages, and the Billy goat appeared to greet them, as if they were old friends.

In November, 1981, Lorelei had an interesting four-hour trip to Ames to meet several of the people connected with the publication of her book. She was treated to lunch at a fine restaurant. They informed her that it would take almost a year before the book would actually be published, but they were busy working on the promotion, marketing and production aspects. Lorelei provided several piles of potential pictures and was informed of the preparatory steps for publication. She was extremely excited for the possibilities of publishing a book that would recognize and honor the devoted people who had made home talent shows possible.

Lorelei was also working on another book: "The Big Five and Some Littler Ones: A Unique Kind of Show-making Business." It would be about the biggest five producing companies, from 1903 to the present. She had received hundreds of letters, tapes and manuscripts to gather material for the book that would be a forgotten aspect of American theatre history. She would include in her travels the research needed for the five companies.

As she traveled for research, Lorelei was able to visit family members also. She made the most of her opportunities for study and leisure.

First, she had a lovely trip to Chicago to the Blackstone Hotel. It was like a once, grand countess who had torn silks, shabby furs and loose teeth. While there, she visited the Chicago Public Library, within the Historical Collection Department and discovered details of T.P. Blackstone's life, for whom the library was named. He was a surveyor for the railroads when they were brought into Chicago in the 1840s. He was later the president of one railroad, and founder and president of the gigantic Union Stockyards. She also read that Carl Sandburg spoke of Chicago as the "hog butcher of the world," and the Union Stockyards with their initial 100 acres, acquired money, bringing animals from farms all over the nation to be slaughtered, packed and shipped out all over the world.

Second, Lorelei took the train, Amtrak, into Chicago and then flew the next day to the Tampa Airport and rented a blue, Ford Mustang. It was a three-hour drive to see her brother, Donald, and her sister, Marty, in Lehigh Acres. One night they had two pounds of delicious steamed shrimp, and another they had a Chinese type dish with squash, all they could eat. At Ft. Myers

Beach, one afternoon they had seafood lunch by the harbor. They went to Sanibel Island for the sunset and to wade their feet in the cool waters. They had an outing at Naples Beach then drove up to Clearwater to attend Church. She had an unusual discussion with her siblings. They told her they had pooled their resources and bought an acre of land and had a number of enterprises planned for it, including a convenience store. Donald informed Lorelei in his husky voice: "I have already made inquiries to Iowa about vegetables that we can purchase for our store!" Lorelei encouraged them both: "Yes, you will find such fine vegetables grown in Iowa, and I am sure your store will be a great success!" She knew her brother had entrepreneur ideas and had attended Emory University and knew he was very intelligent about the business world. She also knew that her sister, Marty, would be a good partner for him, as she was always so encouraging and honest. She wished them well in their endeavors, as she knew they were almost inseparable.

In Florida, one very special highlight of Lorelei's was her visit with the pelicans. They were such dear birds to her! At Sanibel by the edge of the Gulf, she was joined by a bunch of them (only three yards from her), going about their fishing. Another one on nearby rocks tried to take away a fish a man had just caught and was stringing up. When Donald and Lorelei went on a dock by sand flats, a boat pulled up, and a man took out a fish and pretended to conduct a bunch of pelicans, as though he were an orchestra conductor, using the fish as a baton and singing a song, and their necks all swayed in time to the music. Then he threw them the fish. They also saw a smallish variety of sea gulls at the beach.

Third, Lorelei flew to St. Louis by Ozark, and then from St. Louis to Burlington on Britt Airlines. It was quite an experience, as if she was in a toy rather than a real airline, with just one row of seats on either side and so low, one had to stoop to walk down the aisle. There were only six passengers on the plane, and they were practically with the two pilots and could see everything they were doing. Ted met her at the airport. He hugged her in his rough-and-tough way, but Lorelei was so happy to be back home.

Within a couple months, she received a letter from Marty telling her that their enterprises had gone sour, because Donald had decided to enterprise the flea markets instead, which would include traveling to the different markets and setting up booths. He told Marty that he would pay her back with his profits. Marty wrote that she was going to attend a community college and seek a career in drug and alcohol abuse counseling. As Lorelei read her letter, she hoped that her siblings would settle their debts. She shared the letter with Ted. In one discussion, before Eileen and David's visit back in '74, they thought that Marty or Donald could be their heir. At that time, Lorelei tried to tell him that she was not sure that her brother and sister would be interested in farming for life. However, since their decision was crucial for future generations, they would consider all family members.

Chapter Eight:

Co-Author

Although Lorelei was needed most of the time on the farm, Ted realized that she wanted and needed to continue her educational studies, so he agreed that she could volunteer with the community theatre. She became one of the co-founders of the Creston Community Theatre and gave a speech at its first anniversary. She wrote several scripts including one called, "The Bus to Bula Bula," extracted from her European journals. She was finally able to bring her dream of writing about her own experiences in fictional style. It was a comedy, romance play about Dell, a waiter on a cruise ship, who had fallen in love with one of the passengers, Blanche. The bus tour was taking the passengers to the sacred and romantic shrine of Bula Bula. There was a robbery which caused Dell and Blanche to become stranded on the island. Lorelei wrote in the conclusion, that the romance between Blanche and Dell was not destined for permanence, but it helped Dell gain the courage he needed to find a better job. So, she was able to re-live her own experiences through pen.

An intensified breakthrough occurred when Lorelei also volunteered to catalogue scripting for the Museum of Repertoire Americana. There she met Maxine and her husband, William, former journalists, who were interested in writing a book about "Hometown Talent on Stage." They drew Lorelei into their conversations about the research involved in tracing the stories of early 20th century home talent shows, where production companies traveled to different cities and recruited local performers. It was the beginning of a new horizon for Lorelei.

She discussed the conversations that she had with Maxine and William with Ted, and told him how she would have to travel to different cities to conduct her research. She would need to go to Maine and Indiana and cities in Iowa, as they would be writing about the life of a dramatic coach from Fairfield, Iowa. Ted was very supportive, which surprised and delighted Lorelei. It seemed Ted was full of surprises at times.

During her research travels in 1982, Lorelei was able to visit her sister, Donna Marie, and her family in Georgia. It was Summer. As the children were out of school, Lorelei treated her sister and Steve, David and Viki to a grand tour of the High Museum of Art on Peachtree Street in Atlanta. The museum was the leading art museum of the Southeastern U.S. at that time, and Lorelei and David were able to embellish their previous experiences in Paris to some of the Impressionist paintings. David enlightened them with his cultured learning and pointed to the sculptures. He named the artist before anyone could look at the name plaques below. Lorelei elucidated the picture-perfect boxed holly trees on the piazza of *The Art of the Louvre's Tuileries Garden*. Viki, with great excitement, standing next to her Aunt Lorelei whispered, "Oh, how beautiful the holly trees illuminate the orange trees!" Her aunt replied, "Yes, and how lovely it was to sit by the fountains in Paris and watch David, Lara and Stewart throw coins over their heads!" Steve came up behind his aunt and stated in a sentimental tone: "You know, Aunt Lorelei, those coins they threw were for *good luck* wishes for you! They loved you very much for that European opportunity!" She hugged her nephew, and they moved on to the next exhibition.

The five of them enjoyed a fine lunch at the historical Mary Mac's Tea Room, opened after World War II by Mary MacKenzie. Mary Mac's was the epitome of southern cooking with menu selections of tomato pie, fried okra and homemade cornbread. It was rather a humorless ending to a special day with their Aunt Lorelei, as she would be catching the afternoon Greyhound bus back to Iowa. David tried to make light of the situation, as he knew they may not see her again for a long time. Lorelei was traveling and researching for her novel about the home talent shows, and she was very busy on the farm with her husband. So, David told a few more jokes, then related one paradoxical evening in Europe. Lorelei stopped him at first, fearing that he was about to reveal their secret evening in Italy, but he assured her by shaking his head that he was not. David began: "When we played our parts in Shakespeare's play, *Romeo and Juliet*, one evening in England, little did we know that Lara and Stewart would truly play their parts! I saw it in their eyes, and when I nudged my aunt about it, she nodded in agreement, and I remember laughing at the irony. We had no idea that they would fall in love! They were almost complete opposites, one shy and one focused only on studying, and yet, after that evening, we saw a change in them." Lorelei added: "Yes, and David and I felt as if we had been matchmakers, without even knowing it!"

As everyone said goodbye and hugged their aunt at the bus depot, Donna Marie pulled her aside before she walked up the steps. She put her arm around her sister and asked her: "Lorelei, are you truly happy with Ted? Is the farm work too much for you? Is it everything you expected or less?" Her sister reassured her: "Donna Marie, I am fine. It is not really what I expected, but it is my fate. I chose to be with Ted, to help him, to be by his side, working his family's farm. At least, I have been able to write and teach. I tell you honestly, the only small part missing, is the romantic love. But at least I have experienced it." At that remark, Donna Marie stumbled away in embarrassment, as Lorelei chuckled at her sister's coyness. Donna Marie was always the timid and shy one. As Lorelei stepped up to hand the bus driver her ticket, she saluted her Georgia family. They all waved back with blown kisses and told her they loved her. It was like a scene from the movies of a dear one parting for the last time, never to be seen again.

For four years, Lorelei was the chief researcher, as she traveled to thirteen states and wrote over a hundred letters of inquiry to gather material. She discovered that Fran, the dramatic coach, had recorded her adventures for a book project that she never completed, so she was able to use her notes and recordings. Lorelei could relate to Fran's life, especially about being childless. From the *Postscript* in <u>1,001 Broadways Hometown Talent on Stage</u> by Lorelei F. Eckey, Maxine Allen and William T. Schoyer, she noted: "Fran's life expressed the integrity of devotion to one career and making the most she could of it. Home talent was the be-all and end-all for which she journeyed across all the stars in the flag. Each town in which she halted became her hearthstone where she assembled a family for the duration. The older members of the cast were her brothers, sisters, uncles, aunts, parents, grandparents and children she never had."

Lorelei came upon an old magazine with an article that stated Ronald Reagan achieved his beginnings in show business from a home talent show. Lorelei had written to his hometown, but they did not have any information about it. She also wrote directly to President Reagan, and received a response from Anne, who was Director of Correspondence, for the President saying, "It is not possible to comply with your request for more information about the President's involvement in talent shows," and she signed off, "With the President's best wishes and gratitude for your friendship." Lorelei hoped she could go to Dixon, Illinois and spend more time going through old newspapers to find something definite about his show biz beginnings in home talent shows.

It happened by chance that Lorelei received an invitational letter from Joany, one of the descendants of a costume director. Joany asked if she would like to come to Boston to interview her about the costumes they used in one of the home talent production companies. This was Lorelei's chance to possibly see her ex-in-laws again, who had only written her once since her divorce, saying they were sorry they could no longer keep in touch due to the circumstances. She thought she could at least drop by for a visit to see them, and she would call first. She spoke with Ted telling him her intentions, and he cautioned her: "Lorelei, you might not want to run into your ex-husband. It may be too stressful for you to see him again." Ted knew the depth of their marriage relationship, as Lorelei had also shared their overseas post cards written to each other. Lorelei responded in assurance: "I will not see him again. However, I may try to visit his parents."

The following week after accepting Joany's invitation, Lorelei arrived at the Boston airport. She rented a light green Ford Pinto for her travels while in Boston. She booked a room at the Harborside Inn, with its unique, Victorian furnishings and sleigh beds, and its location near Faneuil Hall. She was in familiar territory. She checked in and made a call to Joany to schedule an interview for the next day. She sat on the bed looking in the phone book for her ex-in-laws' phone number. When she found it, she was shaking, as she dialed their number. Fred's mother, Barbara, answered the phone, and Lorelei cleared her soprano throat: "Barbara, Hi. This is Lorelei. I hope I am not calling at a bad time. I happen to be in Boston for business, and I thought perhaps I could see you and Charlie, if that would be convenient, just for a very, short visit." She waited for Barbara's response. She could tell she was a bit surprised to hear from her, as she did not answer right away. She could hear Charlie in the background asking her who was on the phone. Barbara paused, "Lorelei, can you hold for just a moment?" Lorelei said she could. When Barbara came back to the phone, she had obviously told Charlie who it was and what Lorelei had asked. Barbara replied in a soft tone: "Lorelei, we would love to see you again. When can you come by?" So, they scheduled a visit for the next day in the late afternoon.

The next morning, Lorelei went to see Joany for the interview and had a very productive conversation with her about the costumes. She provided journal entries from her aunt about the wardrobes: "mops for wigs, short skirts, long johns, fluffy ballet skirts, balloon bosoms, stilts and makeup gimmicks." She interviewed Joany for two hours for the novel, and then they had a nice, casual conversation of Lorelei's previous years in Boston. She was offered green tea and delicious scones. She thanked her and promised she would give her a complimentary copy of the book when it came out.

By two o'clock, Lorelei drove to her ex-in-laws, remembering the elite Brookline neighborhood, where they had lived for over thirty years. It was second-nature to her. She was greeted kindly by Barbara. They hugged as if it had not been twelve years since they had seen each other. Charlie came out also to hug her, as he remembered fondly what a wonderful daughter-in-law she had been. Lorelei was dressed in a dark blue semi-formal suit with a dark blue scarf and matching pearl earrings. She had wanted to appear as business-like as possible. They both complimented her suit and lovely hair tied in a twist. She told them they both looked wonderful and remembered their elegant home. They offered her to join them for afternoon tea, so they invited her into the adjoining room. Lorelei had not given them much notice, but they had told her she was welcome anytime she was in Boston. They asked if she had remarried. Lorelei began to tell them all about her new life in Iowa with her farmer.

Suddenly, in mid-sentence, she heard laughing, as two people came in the front door, arm-in-arm. It was Fred and Manette! Fred was dressed in a white tennis suit, and so was Manette, looking as handsome, and her as beautiful, as she remembered them. Fred's jaw dropped at least an inch, as he recognized his ex-wife from a dozen years ago! She looked stunning! He gained his balance and held his new wife's hand, as they entered the adjoining room and made their greetings. Fred spoke first in a sincere tone: "Lorelei, what an unexpected pleasure! Manette, you remember our Lorelei?" Manette chimed in: "Oh, Lorelei, it is so good to see you again! How have you been? We have thought about you so often through the years and hoped that you were well and happy!" They all hugged each other, as if it was the natural and appropriate thing to do. They all sat down in a semi-circle on the sofas, and as they chatted about her new life and their new life, Lorelei sensed closure approaching. She could tell that they were very happy together, and it made her heart swell with warmth for them. At that moment, as time seemed to freeze during their candid back-and-forth conversations, she forgave Fred for breaking her heart. They chatted for over an hour, and Lorelei raised up to say she had to leave. They all felt peace that Lorelei had taken the time to visit them. They congratulated her on her upcoming novel, and Manette took her aside for a moment, and personally thanked her. She said tenderly, "Thank you for understanding. Fred and I have been so happy these years together. We were unable to have any children, but we try to give our love to the children in the Church. I do hope you will stay in touch with us and forgive us." Lorelei tearfully whispered in return: "Manette, I do forgive, because I see how happy you both are together. It was meant to be. Sometimes we do not know our Lord's purpose, but today I saw it. Thank you for the closure I needed." Lorelei said her good-byes to Barbara and Charlie and waved to Fred, as she saw him asking Manette what the two of them had been discussing. He would know when she told him. So, Lorelei left her past behind and spent the rest of her evening driving by the historic sites she remembered: Paul Revere's House, The Old North Church, the USS Constitution, Bunker Hill Monument and The Old State House. She packed her bag the next morning and was on the first plane back to Iowa.

Ted greeted her at the airport and could tell she had a meaningful trip. He waited until she wanted to tell him. On their drive home, she told him everything. Ted was thankful that she could finally forgive her ex-husband.

Chapter Nine:

Research Discovery

Finally, Lorelei was able to combine her novel research with her genealogy research. Over the years, she had accumulated vital records for her paternal side of the family, but not as much for her mother's side, until she had the major breakthrough with the maternal grandfather's name. She never gave up hope that she might come across data that would lead her to an explanation for her mother's disappearance. She usually tried historical societies and the local libraries, but she also heard that museums had archives that would also be helpful.

She traveled by car in her Dodge Aries to Flora, Indiana, the hometown of her ancestors. Her great, great grandfather had founded Flora, Indiana, and she had scheduled a visit with a distant cousin, Jeannie, who had unidentified photographs that she hoped Lorelei could help identify. She discovered her new cousin, Jeannie, from another cousin's letter, who had recently passed away. She was meeting her at Denny's. They had corresponded to confirm the direct descent of the same great grandmother, Lucinda. Lorelei was the first at the restaurant and ordered a corner table telling the waitress that they would be staying several hours and hoped that they could have privacy. The waitress was kind and accommodating. Lorelei started to read her menu knowing she would just order a salad and tea. Jeannie arrived while she was looking over the menu, and immediately they recognized in each other the characteristics of the Flora family! They hugged and were so excited to see each other! Lorelei saw that Jeannie brought the large, family album with her. She ordered salad and tea also, and they began talking endlessly for hours. They had so much in common, now that Lorelei was a farmer's wife, as Jeannie was a farmer's wife in Indiana. She told Lorelei she would show her the Flora Farm, that was only a couple miles down the road, before dusk. Sadly, Jeannie told her: "The family farm of course was sold, because no one for years claimed it as their heritage. It was sold to strangers who now own it, but I hear they are a very nice family and have many children." After they finished their salad, they began looking at the photos. They were photos from the 1800's, and Lorelei was ecstatic! This was her dream of finding more photos to include in her ancestor notebooks! Jeannie told her that her own siblings could not identify them, so she figured they were perhaps from Lorelei's side of the family. As she turned the pages, Lorelei clapped in excitement: "Yes, I know who that is! That is our connection! That is our great grandparents, Samuel and Lucinda! They look wonderful! That is why I am a farmer's wife!" The photo showed Samuel with a long beard dressed in a heavy overcoat, and Lucinda in a burlap-type, long dress with matching cape. Her hair was parted in the middle and tied back. Lorelei shared with Jeannie her information about their religion: "They were members of the Dunkard Brethren Church which originated in Germany in 1708. Was your side of the family also Dunkards?" Jeannie nodded in response: "Yes, my research has found that their plainness in dress was from the *Old Order Brethren*." They soon discovered that Lorelei was able to identify most of the photos, so Jeannie surprised her: "Lorelei, the album is yours. I have already made a copy of the photo of Samuel and Lucinda. The other photos must have been from your family branch. It belongs to you and your descendants. It has been so wonderful getting to know you today, and I am thrilled to go back and tell my family what we have discussed!" Lorelei was so thankful but not sure she should accept the album: "Jeannie, I am not sure I should accept. You see, I do not have any children of my own, but I do have a niece who loves genealogy as much as I do, and I know she would continue the legacy! Her name is Viki, so that you will know that she is the connecting future relative. Okay?" Jeannie held out both hands to reach for Lorelei's in conclusion: "Yes, it sounds like Viki will treasure the photos, as you have done! Give me her address sometime, and I will forward it to my children, so they may keep in touch!" They left the restaurant three hours later and tipped the waitress graciously, who kept filling their tea glasses. Lorelei followed Jeannie's car as they drove by the family farm, and it reminded her of Ted's. It was a two-story farmhouse with about a hundred acres and beautiful gardens in the backdrop. She made a mental note to tell Ted all about her visit with Jeannie. They would want to discuss again the issues concerning their heir.

The next day, Lorelei went to the Carroll County Historical Museum, where she discovered even more valuable information about her great grandparents that she would share with Viki. Someone in the family had already submitted photos of Lucinda and Samuel, who were teachers and farmers in Flora. She spent almost the entire day in the museum, and then remembered she still needed to research for the local home talent shows. She went up to the front desk to ask for information of which library would be most beneficial. The woman at the front desk was probably in her early seventies. She was very knowledgeable about the area and told Lorelei she would need to travel to the Indiana Public Library in Indianapolis for that type of research. Lorelei decided since the woman named Stacy was so informative, that she would ask her a few more questions about Flora, Indiana. She told Stacy about her visit with her cousin, Jeannie. She also told her that their ancestors had founded Flora, and she wondered if any of them were still alive in the area. Stacy replied in her very friendly Indiana voice: "Yes, there are a few Flora family members still here. In fact, just last month, I was chatting with a regular visitor to the museum, Mary, and she was talking about her family, and how she wished she could see them again. Mary lives in a nursing home down the street, and she is a little confused sometimes, so I listened as she wanted to talk more about them. She said that she knew from the day of the accident that she was a Flora by marriage. She did not know anything else about her identity, because of her injuries, but she knew she had to get home to Flora, Indiana for some reason." Lorelei stopped her abruptly in apology: "Stacy, what did you say her name was?" Stacy replied, "Mary." Lorelei asked, "What did she look like?" Stacy replied, "She was probably about the same age as me, in my seventies, but you could tell she had some scars and must have lived a hard life. Her hair was white, but she looked as if she was once very beautiful. Do you think you know her?" Lorelei was so excited, she could not stand still. She jumped so high, she startled Stacy: "Stacy, I think that she is my mother, who disappeared from us over 30 years ago! Where is the nursing home?" Stacy matched her excitement and eagerly gave Lorelei the address to the Flora Senior Center, hoping it was her mother. Lorelei told her she would let her know the outcome, thanked and hugged her.

Lorelei stopped off at the nearby Motel 6 to regain her composure and to call Ted of the news. When she excitedly told him the news, he warned her that it may not be her mother, so he did not want her to be heartbroken, if it was not. He told her she should probably wait until the next morning to make her appearance. Lorelei agreed. When she hung up with Ted, she called her sister, Donna Marie, and told her the same news. Donna Marie also cautioned her to not be disappointed if it was not their mother, but to call her the next day after her visit. Donna Marie added: "I will be praying that it is our mother, and that all these years she has been alive!" Lorelei decided not to call her other siblings until she knew more.

The next morning about nine o'clock, Lorelei wore a similar cotton dress to the ones her mother use to buy for her and Donna Marie. She wanted to be able to jog her memory, if needed. She knew she might need proof also to even visit her, so she made sure she had her birth certificate in her purse that she always carried with her. She walked up to the front desk in the small, clean nursing home and asked to see Mary Flora. The nurse behind the desk asked for her relation to Mary, and Lorelei provided her birth certificate. The nurse commented with anticipation: "You will be the first visitor ever for Mary! We all have wondered what happened to her family! I will personally take you to her room!"

In Room 108, Lorelei saw her mother sitting in a rocking chair holding two rag dolls. She had on a pink faded cotton dress, looked a little plump but healthy, and her light gray hair was pulled back on each side with lovely pearl barrettes. The nurse approached first to forewarn Mary that she had a very nice visitor. When Lorelei came forward, she thought her mother was going to faint! The nurse held her up, told her to take a deep breath, and sat her back down on the rocking chair. Lorelei slowly came up to her mother and gently hugged her: "Oh, mother, I have found you! Are you okay?" Lorelei squatted at her mother's feet. It took her mother a few moments to realize who she was. She closed her eyes at first, thinking that she was dreaming. Then she reopened them, when she felt Lorelei's hands in her own. Tears came down her cheeks, as she remembered: "Oh, my daughter, Lorelei. I have missed you so much. Where is Donna Marie? Where are Donald and Marty? Where is your father? There are so many questions to ask!" Lorelei reassured her mother that there was plenty of time to answer all her questions. She offered her a glass of water and motioned to the nurse that she could probably leave them alone. It would be okay.

For the next two hours, with several breaks for water, Lorelei answered her mother's questions. She also told her that her father had remarried and passed away in 1976 of a heart attack. When she finished the updates, she asked her mother if she was prepared to tell her what happened on that mysterious day she disappeared. She nodded yes.

Her mother took another deep breath and began: "As you may remember, I told you I was going to the movies. I remembered feeling intimidated more than usual that day by your father, and he and I had talked about a divorce. So, I just needed to get out of the house. I had on one of my cotton dresses and a sweater, and I had my purse with just a few dollars in it for the show. When I saw that the movie was a scary one, I decided I would just walk through the park instead. It was a clear, cool day, so I was enjoying the leisure so much, I decided to keep walking past the park. I had so many thoughts running through my mind. I thought about my husband's intelligence and passion for learning, and how you had taken after him. I thought of Donna Marie, and how she was more like me as a dreamer. She loved to play with her toy soldiers and paper dolls. Donald and Marty were so much trouble. They were like twins. I never had any time for myself or time with my husband. I remembered that before you were all born, our romantic evenings were slow and special, and he made me feel so beautiful. I thought of myself in a mousetrap, because economics would not allow us to separate. Of course, your father could find another woman, maybe someone younger and more intelligent than me. I was feeling so sorry for myself, that I did not realize I had completely crossed Detroit to the docks for Belle Isle Park. The sun was going down. I could see rain clouds in the sky. I began to panic. In my purse, I found a few coins, but I knew I had no identification, if I was stopped by police, as a woman wondering the streets alone. I needed to find a pay phone to call your dad to pick me up. It started raining heavily. I could hardly see across the street, but I thought I saw a pay phone. I saw no car coming, so I ran towards it in excitement. However, I remember hearing and seeing, out of nowhere, a red Ford Mustang swing around the corner. I knew I was going to be hit. It must have knocked me to the pavement flat. I learned from the doctors later that the man in the mustang immediately stopped and ran to my side. I was unconscious. He ran to the same pay phone I had attempted, and he called for an ambulance. He was frantic, until the emergency crew arrived and clarified to him, that I was still alive. The emergency crew thought they recognized the man to be the famous ballplayer, Hank Greenberg, but they were never sure. He insisted he ride with me to the hospital. He also requested that no police report be written. He may have given them some money for that request. They agreed, as there was no identification found for me, and I was listed as "Jane Doe" having a road accident on a slippery street near the docks. The man waited at the hospital, until he knew for sure that I would survive. The head doctor told him that I had a concussion and possible memory loss, but that all of my other vital signs were fine. So, he left, but not before he gave an envelope to the head doctor, who swore anonymity, a check for $13,000.00 for my medical expenses and future care."

Her mother took sips of water, and then continued: "The doctors told me that I woke in a hospital bed not knowing who I was, or what had happened to me. They gave me what information they knew. When I gained my strength, I begged the head doctor to send me somewhere to live with the money the anonymous donor had given me. The doctor was hopeful that my memory would return someday. The doctor and hospital staff met to discuss my case and "Jane Doe" cases before me. A semi-type of mental facility was usually the protocol. One of my regular nurses told me that during my sleep, she heard a recurring word, "Flora." It struck her as coincidental, because she was from Flora, Indiana. She suggested to the doctor, and I agreed, to send me to a facility in Indiana. The nurse, Maria, persuaded the head doctor to let her travel with me to the facility chosen near Flora. So, after only seven days in the hospital, I was released to Maria, and she and I travelled to Indiana. Maria took care of everything, including assigning me a caretaker for the money remaining from my benefactor. Of course, I found out later that the money ran out, and I officially became a Ward of the State. But Maria made sure I had everything I needed at that time, and she promised to visit me often.

It took over six years to regain my memory. It happened when I played the piano one day in the mess hall, and suddenly I was playing, by ear, the song that your father sang to me: "Mary's A Grand Old Name," by George M. Cohan. I knew all the notes! My memory came back gradually, after that moment. I realized my name, and that I had left my family." Mary stopped, and Lorelei reached up to her hug her mother. They wept together.

Mary then told her that she asked herself questions: "Should I go back to my family? Would my girls be married or in college by now? Would my husband have remarried? It had been over six years. I decided to stay. I had so many new friends who needed me, and I was able to serenade them with my piano genius! Recently, I was moved to this home. And now, it has been almost 30 years? Look at how beautiful you are, Lorelei! I have missed you so much! I am so sorry!"

Lorelei was completely stunned by her mother's story. It took several minutes to digest. When she did, all she could think of to say was: "I am here now, mother, and I will take care of you. Please come live on the farm with Ted and me." Her mother slowly shook her head adamantly: "I cannot leave. I am comfortable here. But I would love to have visitors!" Somehow Lorelei understood, even though it seemed strange not to take her mother back with her. She promised her mother she would let everyone know that she was safe, and soon she would have visitors. Lorelei stayed a few more hours and ate lunch with her mother, as Mary introduced her family in the cafeteria. She had many friends, and it looked as if she was happy. Lorelei also talked with the office manager and provided extra funds for her mother's comfort. She kissed her mother on the cheek and told her she would be back soon, and that she loved her. She had never given up on finding her. Her mother concluded: "Somehow, Lorelei, I knew your special intelligence would find me. I love you, too, and please tell Donna Marie, I love her, too, and Marty and Donald."

Lorelei drove by the library to thank Stacy. Stacy was anxious to hear the outcome. Lorelei, in exhaustion, exclaimed: "Stacy, she looked wonderful and although, she did not recognize me at first, it only took a few minutes, and then she told me her story. It was heartbreaking!" Lorelei gave her a summary of her mother's disappearance, and how she ended up in Flora. Stacy listened with sincere interest, and when Lorelei had finished, she said a prayer of thanks: "I am so pleased that she is your mother, and that she came in here often to check out classics and talk to me. The Lord wanted her to finally be found by her family!" Lorelei gave Stacy a hug and told her she was indeed the Lord's messenger.

When she returned to the motel, she made her phone calls. She first called her sister and told her everything! Donna Marie promised she would make travel plans immediately to visit their mother. Ted was thankful that Lorelei had offered to bring her home to live with them, but he too, seemed to understand that she was probably better off staying in her comfort zone. Lorelei made a brief call to Marty and Donald, but told them she would call them with more details when she returned to Iowa. Lorelei also called her Half-Aunt Dora in Detroit. Dora confessed: "I am so sorry that I have not written to you or Donna Marie all these years, and I did not even try to find out what happened to your mother. I was so ashamed, because I had never married or had any children, so how could I give advice?" Lorelei assured her that all was forgiven. Dora said she was too feeble to travel, but at least she could write a long-overdue apology letter.

Lorelei was satisfied that everyone would visit her in the upcoming years. It was such a relief to know the mystery had been solved. Her mother was healthy and probably would live to be a hundred years old!

Yearly visits were indeed made to Mary. Donna Marie and Lorelei sometimes met each other there, and Donald and Marty always traveled together to see her. Of course, they brought other family members to meet her also. At first, the visits were awkward and strange, having to break the ice of so many years. But then, routine set in, and an accepting fact that their mother had missed 30 years of their lives. They understood the circumstances. However, it was a little more difficult for Donald and Marty, as they hardly even knew their mother, since they had been so young. It was not known, if they ever truly forgave their mother for her choice to not return, once she regained her memory. Perhaps, their visits were out of obligation and respect for a mother, who at least gave them birth.

When Lorelei told her mother about her discovery of her father, Mary, had a breakdown. Her mother had always told her that her father left when she was born. The realization that her own father also abandoned her, as she had her children, was just too much for her. The nurses came in, when they heard her wailing. It took some time to calm her down, and Lorelei had to leave. It was one visit she should have waited for Donna Marie to join her, as she could have helped her tell the story better. By the time, she told her mother the discovery of his name, and that he had remarried and had another daughter, she was in hysterics.

Lorelei went to the nursing home the following day and found her mother recovering. The head nurse pulled her aside and asked what happened to cause her breakdown. Lorelei guiltily admitted: "I told my mother about the father she never knew. I am so sorry. I did not realize how fragile she was." The nurses told her a little more about her medical record: "Yes, we can show you her records now that we know you are her daughter. Her records show that through the years, there have been several major breakdowns, especially when she was in the Central State Hospital. They seemed to happen when she had nightmares about family members. She is a Ward of the State, as you know, and we have a responsibility to her care. She is heavily medicated at this time."

Lorelei studied her mother's medical records. They showed a history of mental breakdowns. Perhaps, that confirmed her decision to choose a simple life, where she would not have the responsibilities of raising a family. Lorelei concluded in her own thoughts that her mother was where she should be for the remainder of her lifetime.

Chapter Ten:

New York

One of the thirteen states that Lorelei included in her travels was Maine. She visited in the Spring Season and stayed at a lovely inn that had antique characteristics. Enkindled memories ignited within her heart, as she drove her Volkswagen rental car along the coast of Maine. Not only the coast but the quaint shops and galleries at Kennebunkport's Dock Square and Village blurred her eyes in tears. She could relate her lonely heart to the lonesome lighthouses in the distance. The beautiful lilacs also reminded her of the colorful tulips of Holland. She knew she would be flying back through New York, so she decided that she would bring closure to her restless heart. She would visit the Solomon R. Guggenheim Museum and make a final view of the Italian Art and Special Exhibition that she had read was on display: "An American Perspective," 1982 Exxon International Exhibition. Perhaps seeing some of the Italian collections that she knew Humberto would have collected also, would help her find some hint that he was alive, had remarried and was happy.

Before she made her airline reservations for a flight to New York with a four-and-a-half-hour layover, she made a few brief visits to descendants of the home talent show coaches for more research. One special visit was to the nephew, Jacob, of one of her main characters, Fran. He was able to provide Lorelei several photos and journal entries that his mother had kept that described the talent shows' travelling companies. His wife, Samantha, prepared an unusual Maine dish for Lorelei. In all of her travels, she had never eaten such a delicious, unusual meal. Samantha boiled the brown bread, baked the kidney beans and grilled the red hot dogs. Lorelei asked for second helpings! She thanked her host and hostess and left Maine. She was satisfied that she had accumulated enough research to type and send to her collaborators for their study and review.

Arriving in New York, Lorelei had ample time to tour the Exhibition. She took a cab to the Guggenheim and immediately walked in to find the displays. She felt especially pretty and at her leisure, dressed in a slinky, green long skirt and white silk buttoned blouse with a rainbow scarf around her neck. She was also wearing her favorite satin shoes that were always so comfortable for her tiny feet. It was like she was in her own little world in animation, as she passed by the seven young Italian painters and sculptors and read each artist's statement, bio and essay in context of their work to the American Perspective.

As she was nearing the end of her personal tour, she imagined a smell of Italian citron cologne and a smoky Italian voice in her right ear whispered: "Mi Mancano i tuoi occhi." Someone was telling her that he missed her eyes. She turned around. It was not her imagination! He held a bouquet of red and white chrysanthemums and carnations in his hand, as he had remembered the corsage he saw her wearing that night at the museum when they first met. It was Humberto in the flesh! She gasped in a return whisper: "Oh, Humberto! They are beautiful! How did you possibly know I might be here?" They hugged each other in front of artist enthusiasts nearby and tried to control their excitement. He motioned for them to step outside, so they could talk. As she put her arm in his, he escorted her out of the museum into the front, where they could sit on a stone bench. She admired his handsome, dark green suit. Underneath the suit jacket, she could see his silk pale, green shirt and gold-colored tie. They looked into each other's eyes.

Lorelei did not wait for his response, she was so excited: "Oh, Humberto, you look so well! Your hair has a touch of handsome gray, and you still look like Sean Connery!" Humberto gave her the familiar, sexy laugh: "I came to find you, my beautiful! My only hope has been that you might visit such an exhibit. I have been attending an exhibition every Spring, holding these flowers, just in case you remembered that I wanted to see New York. This is my seventh visit! My prayers have been answered!" It just occurred to her, when he said *prayers*, that he was probably a Christian after all! There was so much to discuss, so many questions to ask, but at that moment, they embraced and kissed a tender kiss in view of hundreds of people. They felt as if they were the only two people on earth, and they held each other for a long time. Humberto broke the embrace in concern: "Lorelei, how are you? You look as lovely as ever, but your eyes look tired. Is the farm life healthy for you? Are you working too much? Have you become the writer you wanted to be?" So, they talked about her life with Ted, the hard work and the animals. He only interrupted to ask her if she had time to have dinner. She told him she would not be able to do so. She had to catch her plane to Iowa in a few hours. So, she continued her saga and told him she was on the verge of becoming a co-author. She told him the travelling and research that gave her the opportunities of freedom that she needed to survive the hardships of the farm. Then it was his turn. They held hands as lovers, and he told her that his research of art collections was his entire life. He had no time or desire to remarry. He had recently acquired some unusual art pieces from the first millennium BC, so he tried to describe them to her using theatrical gestures. She was entranced! He told her humbly: "Our shop is becoming one of the most exclusive Italian Art Collection shops in the area! I have even been invited to speak at art exhibits and museums!" I would have never thought it possible to achieve my dreams before I was sixty!"

The next remark he made surprised and complimented Lorelei: "There is no other woman for me than you, Lorelei. If I cannot have you, and I know cannot, I will die happy just knowing that you are safe and content in Iowa. We had the most magical evening of our lives. Time is such a strange place, because I feel just seeing you today, that evening is alive again for both of us, and that is all we will ever need." Again, they kissed, and Lorelei let him lead her to his Chevrolet Monte Carlo rental car that was parked behind the museum. They slid together into his rental car like two young teenagers at the drive-in movie. Humberto rolled up the dark-tinted windows and began kissing Lorelei with intensity. As they were embracing, he accidentally tore the top two buttons of her white silk blouse. His breath was racing to the silhouette of her firm round breasts, and he sighed: "My love, I know I cannot touch. You have to climb back on *Your Rock* and not let me *lure you* to temptation. I will admire you only from a distance." He straightened to a sitting position, and then he gently raised Lorelei. She reached in her purse for safety pins, and he pinned her buttons. They both knew they could not go any further. They also knew they did not need to. Their love was more in depth than a sexual communication of two bodies. It was rooted from within their hearts and eyes of their souls. It would be enough for another lifetime without each other.

Humberto offered to drive her to the airport, and she accepted. He provided updated news of his brother still working in his store, then she gave him updates of her trio: "Lara and Stewart are married, and Lara is a photographer, and Stewart is an architect! My nephew married a farmer's wife! Eileen is a preacher, and David has just finished his Bachelor's in Agriculture!" Humberto had listened with great interest in her trio's updates and responded: "I am so glad that your teenagers have grown up to be very successful and happy! You know I really would have loved to have been a relative of your wonderful family!" Lorelei blushed and changed the subject: "Where have you travelled recently?" He responded, "I have travelled mostly in Italy." The next thing he asked her made her very sad: "Will you ever be able to return to Europe?" She looked down, her eyelashes twitching: "I do not think I will ever be back. Ted is very lenient of my U.S. travels, but he would be devastated if I ever told him I was going to Europe again." She confessed to Humberto, looking up into his eyes, that Ted looked at her sometimes, perhaps wondering if there was someone else and was she thinking of him. She told him of the time that Ted asked her questions about Italy, about naming her kittens after the Italian comic performers, and she knew then that Ted did not want to know what happened in Italy. Humberto was hanging on her every word and inferred how Ted must have felt. Lorelei confessed: "I thought if I ever saw you again, I could never say this, but I do truly love my husband. Of course, it is not the intensity of our infinite love, but it is in the realm of a love filled with honor and respect for my farmer." Humberto sincerely understood and agreed: "Yes, it is as it should be. When you made your decision that evening in Italy, it was a commitment I knew you would pursue and esteem."

They reached the John F. Kennedy airport, and he insisted on walking her to the gate. Arm-in-arm, they walked together like two statues held in time, knowing they would probably never see each other again. As the announcement came to board, Humberto looked one final time into her tearful, emerald eyes, and he kissed both eyes tenderly. He whispered, "I love you forever, my Lorelei. My offer is for eternity. I am yours." Lorelei put down her purse and flight voucher, held his face with both of her hands and replied, "My love, I love you more than life itself. I am so thankful for the one evening that our souls met for eternity. Goodbye, my Humberto." In slow motion, as if the video was switched to reverse, and the final kiss was recorded for a re-play, Humberto drew her close and gave Lorelei the immortal kiss.

She was back to Iowa by evening and met her husband, Ted, at the airport. As he kissed her lightly on the lips and looked into her eyes, he asked: "How far did you get in your research?" She answered absentmindedly, "Oh, in Maine, I was able to visit with several of the coaches' descendants from the home talent shows. I will tell you more later. We better get home." Ted did not ask her any more questions, but it was always perplexing when she blew off their conversations. There was something from her past he was not telling her.

Chapter Eleven:

The Economy

In 1982, severe recession began in the U.S. Unemployment was the highest since the Great Depression. The 1973 oil crisis and 1979 energy crisis had a severe effect on savings' accounts. Lorelei and Ted's savings account was at its lowest ever, so a small miracle occurred when Lorelei's research paid off. Iowa State University Press was the publisher. Lorelei became the co-author of the first book to give a notable account of the home talent show, using first-person witnesses and real-life narratives. Although it did not become a bestseller, it provided a few thousand that was needed. Lorelei was interviewed by an editor of the Creston

Iowa Daily Advertiser, and presented the book to the Creston Community Theatre and public library at the opening of Creston's Book Fair.

Lorelei provided another publisher an article about her book. It was called: "Survival in a Peripatetic Depression Days Theatre: The Rogers Company of Fostoria, Ohio," and hoped it would be published in the Theatre Journal. Reflective from these articles, Lorelei had found her comfort zone amidst the throes of a farmer's wife.

Lorelei wrote letters to her sister, Donna Marie, as often as she could, because she knew her sister always worried about her. In February, she wrote: "When the wind was blowing for two days steadily during the ground blizzard—from the northwest, we just could not get the most of the house warm. When I went upstairs to find a cot to put in the kitchen to sleep on (since our bedroom was too cold to sleep in despite insulation and storm windows), my hands nearly froze! But we kept our kitchen cozy.

Ted brought his lazy boy chair in the kitchen to sleep in it, while I pulled my cot next to the oven, still emitting some heat from the extra baking I had done that day to supplement our electric heating system." Donna Marie always appreciated her sister's detailed farm reports through her letters, as she prayed she would survive the harsh weather in Iowa.

Lorelei wrote another letter to her sister about the cool, Fall-like weather: "I am still getting scads of raspberries and have learned to be quite fearless about the huge black and yellow spiders that reside in the brambles by the dozens or more getting fact on the insects that love raspberries. Today I made a sauce of raspberries, elderberries (another very plentiful crop this year), and blue damson plums (from a bunch I picked over at the pasture—not as abundant as usual)." Donna Marie could read-between-the-lines of her letters, knowing that Lorelei was over-working to fill the void for something, but she did not know what had occurred in

Europe. In her return letters, she never asked her sister to reveal her void. She had never even questioned her daughter to see if she knew about her aunt's void, even though she knew her daughter had made a solo visit to her aunt several years ago. She felt that when her sister wanted to tell her, she would.

In her Thanksgiving letter to Donna Marie, she wrote that she had taken a tax course before the holiday that cost her vacation money she had saved. However, it helped her to sort out their farm records that had piled up over the years, including the years Ted had been married to Cleo. She also learned about tax savings that seemed so frightening before. She had planned to see Donna Marie that holiday, so in her letter she apologized she would not be able to visit after all.

In 1983, Ted and Lorelei tried to protect their tomatoes and had been gathering the chickens into the henhouse instead of letting them run wild as they had all Summer. Lorelei called it "The Great Chicken

Roundup." They had been at it every evening for a half hour or so for the past six days and still did not have them all. The chickens were catchable after dark when they roost, but the big problem was discovering where they all were roosting and catching them. Their oldest dog, Bernard, was very helpful, because he was intensely fond of chickens and found them and pointed his nose at them until they found where he was pointing. That worked fine except when he pointed under the floorboards of the barn, and they could not crawl under.

One night in the semi-dark of the barn, Lorelei saw what she took to be the silhouette of a roosting chicken up on a panel and reached for its legs (the way she caught them), and it moved out of her way. So, Lorelei turned on the barn light to see where it had gone, and the "it" turned out to be a rather sizeable possum, white-faced, long tail (somewhere between a cat and dog size). He was wary, rather than afraid of her, and possums did not move fast. So, he and Lorelei just looked at each other until slowly he began to slink away. However, there were still some chickens out: A hen and her almost, grown chick escaped from them the previous evening. They ate grain with the young bull and rams in the daytime. Three of the six half-grown chicks that had been roosting in a tall mulberry tree near the henhouse, were out of reach of human arms.

In February of 1983, Lorelei was on the Iowa Public Television half-hour show called "Touchstone" which aired all over the state on a Thursday evening and again on a Saturday evening. The television studio looked like a large, regular stage and backstage area. When Lorelei arrived, the make-up woman applied special television makeup to her face. She looked radiant! Lorelei also autographed her book for Pat, the star of the show, and the producer, Tom. After her appearance on the television show, Lorelei drove to the brand new studios of the radio station WHO that was heard over a five-state area. It was a controversial station and at that time in a controversial situation, because the President and Congress were talking about the probability of establishing a Radio Mardi beamed down to Cuba which would sue the same frequency WHO used. Castro had vowed to jam it if they did, and he had already illustrated that he could jam that frequency. That would make WHO only effective for about 30 miles, and people in Southeastern Iowa would no longer be able to get it. Show hostess, Julie, interviewed Lorelei about her book for a show to be aired on Saturday morning called, "We Are All Working Women."

When Lorelei and Ted went to the sales barn to sell some of their rams they did not need, the Ringmaster turned around to the Auctioneer and said, "This is Lorelei's ram, and she was on television last week. It lasted a whole half hour!" The auctioneer stopped the sale, wanted to talk with her about it before everyone, and Lorelei would have a good opportunity to sell more of her books, but she was too embarrassed and felt it was not an appropriate place. She shook her head modestly, and he went on with the sale. Afterwards, she brought him a pamphlet about her book that she happened to have in her purse.

By December of that year, Lorelei wrote to her sister about Ted. She added it to the P.S. Closure: "When I tell Ted some times that he is stubborn, he says no, he's not stubborn, just 'firm of purpose.' But there is some Missouri mule in him sometimes. Maybe in most husbands!!!! When he was young, a stunt flier came around the farm and gave him airplane rides, but since then he has never flown anywhere and refuses to do so. He says it is a waste of money, since one gets to see much more when one travels on the ground, and on the ground one has some control of the situation." Lorelei was explaining to her sister that Ted would never travel too far away from his farm. He was a thorough-bred.

They had finished their early lambing and had some fine, large lambs. At first they were all single female, but later they were mostly twins and still mostly female. The previous year they had more males, so it balanced out. Ted had lots of mild weather the past Winter to putter around, and one thing he did was convert an old corncrib into another "barn" for the ewes with new lambs. They seemed to like it. When they fed the ewes, that make enough space for the races to begin – the whole bunch of 23 lambs ran in a group as fast as their little legs could carry them back and forth, with great clamor and joy. They were so cute!

Lorelei was also working on another novel with the working title, "A Fountain Sealed." It was about the legend of *The Trevi Fountain* that she had related to the teenagers, when they had thrown coins into the fountain back in '69. She was again fictionalizing her life through pen. She had so many notes and ideas to choose from her journals!

Ted and Lorelei enjoyed listening to Dick's program, "The Book Shelf," that was on in the mornings during breakfast hours. One particular book that was discussed on the radio intrigued Ted, the non-romanticist. The book was called, "Cold Sassy Tree," by Olive Ann Burns, which was a romance novel set in a small Georgia town. Lorelei laughed silently, as Ted listened intently.

In 1984, the abundance of rain made everything prosper, including the crops. They had lots of strawberries from their garden every night for supper and some to freeze and have for breakfast. Ted liked huge helpings five times the size of normal ones! They also had quite a few cherries from their cherry tree. There were also mulberries. In the garden, they had more lettuce than they could manage, plus radishes, onions and peas.

Lorelei expanded her horizon for her European experiences and wrote a political article for *The Christian Science Monitor*, submitted from her own Macintosh computer that was the first on sale that year. She wrote: "It shocks me that someone has fixed the U.S. 'poverty level' at over $9,000 a year for a family of four, and that everyone under that level is thought of as poor. Is it not true that in some underdeveloped countries the average per capita income is much lower? In India, I remember many people who slept on mats on the public sidewalks and then, on those same mats by day, sold wares to the public. Any of them would have thought themselves millionaires to receive even a fraction of our 'poverty level' wage." It was representative again of her valuable journal entries from her travels around the world and of her compassion for those she had met.

Lorelei also wrote several articles about the home talent shows between 1982 and 1984. One was in the Mt. Pleasant's *The News* entitled, "Home Talent Shows Cut Loose in Mt. Pleasant After War." It read: "By 1921, the local citizens in these shows seemed to be cutting loose, enjoying music and each others' company, joking, laughing, and yet making money, too, for a worthy cause. They were still, sort of, remembering the heroes of the Great War. But they were also putting something between them and the horrific memories."

In her article, "Home Talent Shows in the 20s Were Snappy" for the <u>Missouri Historical Review</u>, of the 1930-1960 Missouri talent shows, she wrote: "The show was *Don't Park Here*, a clever two-act music comedy given January 20-21, 1927. The story concerned a young woman who has aspirations to marry a count. There were between 175 and 200 people in it of the Moorehead Producing Company, headed by relatives of the famous actress, Agnes Moorehead. It was one last nod, one might say, to the fading cluster of memories about America's last great crisis, occurring just a few weeks before the stock market crash."

In 1984, Ted's niece and her father joined Ted and Lorelei at their Church and had dinner afterwards. They discussed how

Lorelei and Ted had attended the annual meeting banquet in Burlington of the State's Historical Society. It rotated around the state to different towns each year. The Society's president showed slides about how Burlington's history was shaped by its hilly location and the fact that the Burlington line railroad found it an ideal place to anchor its line along the Mississippi. At their table at the banquet, Lorelei told the story: "At our table was the former governor of Iowa and his wife—delightful people. Governor Irby had been Governor before I came here, though, and I didn't know who he was until someone told me. A priest at the table who teaches at a college in Davenport, and I both told the people at the table about our books and research, and it was a very interesting night. The banquet facilities were chaired by a friend of mine, who is and had been for some time, the history instructor at the community college where I taught several years ago!" Whenever Lorelei told a story, her listeners were always attentive of the dramatic way she told her stories.

In the Summer of 1984, it was very unusual for Ted to travel out of his home state, but Ted wanted to attend the reunion in Illinois of Ted's first wife, Cleo. Lorelei was okay with attending, and it turned out to be rather interesting. They were invited to share the catfish that had been caught from the Mississippi and to take part in the festivities. One lady had crocheted dishcloths for all the women in attendance, which included Lorelei. Another lady had crocheted little "hats" which were supposed to go on the tops of opened jars, but Lorelei sent her hats to her niece in Georgia, for her future daughter.

In her January, 1985 article, "Shades of Empire: Beach-De Haven Home Talent Shows in Missouri" for the <u>Missouri Historical Review</u>, she wrote: "During their existence, home talent show production companies provided communities in Missouri and elsewhere with professionalized amateur entertainment."

Lorelei also wrote an article entitled, "Pilgrims of the Impossible," in *The Palimpsest*, a publication of the Iowa Historical Society, regarding the "Universal Producing Company," an organization who hired coaches to direct the local performances.

Lorelei wrote a comedy play called, "Take Me, Too," a drama about a husband who had aspirations to be an archeologist, and a wife, who wanted to be an artist. They both wanted to study in Europe, but the husband's parents had other ideas for them. Without his parents' financial support, they would be unable to afford Europe, so the play had a comical twist of persuading the parents. Lorelei submitted her manuscript to the Creston Community Theatre.

As her plays and articles endorsed, Lorelei showed satisfaction that she had achieved her dreams to be a researcher and writer. She had also survived the unthinkable, as a sheep farmer's wife. The only dream at deficit was Italian eyes and a child of her own. Could her God-son and his wife supersede that deficit?

In November 1985, Ted and Lorelei finalized their Will, after several pre-discussions with Ted's brother and niece. They came to an agreement with Ted and Lorelei's choice for heir. In the Will, Ted made sure that Lorelei was his primary beneficiary. If Ted passed away first, Lorelei would be the heir, and she had the right to leave it to any of her descendants, including either of her sisters, her brother, either of her nephews or her niece. If Lorelei happened to pass away before Ted, he agreed to honor the decision for heir they had made together. He would turn it over to that descendant, and he would move into a nursing home. Weighing their options, they knew that David's Agricultural Degree and learned knowledge in planting seeds and shearing sheep, and Eileen's years of hands-on farming experience would be crucial in their decision to carry on Ted's family legacy. Yet, they also knew that Viki was in college studying to be a teacher as Lorelei had done and was more like Lorelei than anyone else in the family. Lorelei hoped that even her sister, Donna Marie, could possibly live on the farm with them, as she was still a widow, and she would probably want to live with her youngest, Viki, and her future husband, Albert. Steve was obtaining his Master's Degree in Business Management, so he would have the economic knowledge needed for the farm, and Patricia, in her licensed ministry, would provide the community with the Christian love and faith needed for success. Marty was almost finished with a Degree in Abuse Counseling, and Donald was street-smart and knew the ins-and-outs of selling all types of ware. There was a family reunion in Georgia planned for the following year in 1986. At that time, they would disclose their choice.

Chapter Twelve:

The Accident

By 1985, President Reagan at the age of 73, took the oath for his second term of office and signed the Federal Debt Recovery Act, that would provide collection services of indebtedness owed the U.S.

In July, Ted sold six of Lorelei's sheep. They were down to 29 ewes, six rams and eleven deer feeder lambs. Ted had sold off the cattle that he would have fed all Winter to lighten his load, but he still had lots of cows and calves and three bulls.

Lorelei also was no longer an amateur at canning. She canned applesauce that took lots of peeling and chopping and time. She would have preferred working on her novels instead. But she prided herself on the art of canning that she had achieved. With the last two batches, she mixed in raspberries and elderberries for a pretty pink color.

By the Fall of 1985, they had a pair of Chinese white geese, the nicest-tempered geese they had ever owned. The female had laid eggs in the Spring. Their six goslings were bigger than the chickens and taller. They would all greet each other by bowing their long necks down to the ground in some sort of ritual, reminding Lorelei of how the China men bowed low to greet someone. Since they were Chinese geese, she wondered if the Chinese learned to greet each other by copying the way their geese did!

"Old Threshers" was always five days ending in Labor Day, and each year, Ted would work at the information desk in the Crafts Building, and Lorelei was the guide for the Theatre Museum. Lorelei also attended the annual meeting of the Society for the Preservation of Folk, Tent and

Repertoire Theatre. She learned about showboats and wanted to write a novel about them also someday. She and Ted read lots of books together about the Ohio and Mississippi Rivers, where the showboats traveled. They read one together called, <u>Voices on the River</u>, the story of the Mississippi Waterways by Walter Havighurst. They also sent off for a book from a Canadian book store advertised in the *Monitor* that sold dozens of sheep books. It was about raising sheep in the Welsh Mountains around Snowden called, <u>I Bought a Mountain</u>, by Thomas Firbank.

They were thinking of going on Labor Day to Bethel, Missouri, to the International Sheep Festival. However, they did not make it in time, but drove up to Waterloo instead for the Annual Cattle Congress. It was where they had attended fifteen years ago when they were first dating, so it was kind of an anniversary for them. They went especially to see the sheep show, because Ted was hoping he would be able to persuade someone there to sell him a small ram to service their younger ewes. There was not a sheep auction, but he went around the pens and talked to people, and there were more sheep there than Lorelei had seen at almost any other show she had attended. Ted found and purchased a dear little Cheviot ram (produced by selection rather than crossing), a pure breed, so that when the Cheviot ram was mated with crossbred ewes of other breeds, he would produce superior characteristics of Cheviotness to his offspring. The Cheviot ram was also distinctive in his appearance with his head carried high, absent of wool and absence of horns that marked an aristocratic feature. His head, legs and ears were covered with fine, white hair. Above all, he was strong, vigorous and alert with a quick, coordinated stride. Lorelei named him, Hercules.

The Cattle Congress was interesting, though they did not begin or try to see everything. They watched a display of horses and Calvary soldiers perform cavalry drills and fighting techniques, and some of them were very exciting, much more so than on the movie screen, when they go after the Indians, because they were live and so close. The army was in evidence there in several other events, in a mountain climbing demonstration using a tall box high in the air on fifty-foot-high stilts, and a parachuting one that had Lorelei holding her breath. A plane would eject parachuters who would free-fall in formation carrying purple jet-stream-like markers so the crowd could see them, and when they thought they would not be able to open their chutes, they did, and they landed right near everyone. There was a "hall of breeds" in which they displayed live animals of many of the main breeds of cattle, horses, sheep and goats. There was also a building in which, in a glass case, they had a life-size cow and calf carved entirely of butter. There were many other exciting commonly finds at a fair including the carnival, food tents, machinery displays, spinners and weavers. Lorelei enjoyed getting out and traveling away from the farm during those times.

In the Autumn of that year, Lorelei wrote a letter to Donna Marie about an injury. She wrote: "The leaves were so exquisite that morning! I decided I would walk the entire grounds of the farm, before doing my chores. I was wearing my working jeans and sweat shirt, but I had decided to wear only my tennis shoes, instead of my working boots, so I could be more comfortable walking the distance. I felt at peace with my surroundings, with my life, with my accomplishments as a writer and author and with my husband. I remembered how I felt on the Amalfi Coast, the feeling of déjà vu, and the feeling of "home." I felt the same on the farm, except that it was a different "home" feeling. It was a "Christian home" feeling. Italy was a "romantic home feeling" of emotions and love. The farm was a feeling of moral righteousness and goodness. With those thoughts, I had come to a crossroads, and it felt wonderful! I was so happy! I walked by the cows and bulls and waved to Humbert, as if to say goodbye. I walked by the sheep and waved to Hercules and Christie Lee. I said, 'good morning' to each animal. I loved all the animals. You remember Bernard, our faithful dog, who was missing that day you and Viki were visiting? Even though he had been Ted's dog from the beginning, he seemed to think I needed more protection, so he always followed me around. I came out of my reverie. I needed to do my chores. As I made it to the chicken house next to the barn, I noticed a huge pile of chicken manure which was piled up for the fertilizer process. I was in my usual routine. I could have done my chores blindfolded, and I just shook my head at the huge piles, knowing they were not in the usual locations that Ted would have put them. He had recently hired a part-time, older man from the Church to shovel the manure. He was a little hard of hearing and must not have heard Ted correctly of where to place the piles."

"It was an accident, of course. I was humming the tune from the musical *Oklahoma* of "Oh, What a Beautiful Mornin,'" by Richard Rodgers and Oscar Hammerstein II. I began gathering eggs from the chicken coop, singing to the chickens my song, but as I walked out of the coop, I tripped over Bernard, not seeing him underneath. If I had worn my boots, they would probably have blocked the fall. My whole body fell flat on one of the huge piles of manure. My face was covered with the nasty stuff, and my ankle felt numb. Bernard, poor thing, kept barking at me, as if he wished he could pick me up. I spit out as much as I could but had no rag to wipe my mouth. I stayed on the ground a few minutes and tried to get up, but I could not! I also knew that Ted was on the other side of the pasture, so I would have to make the effort to get up by myself. I tried to instruct Bernard to go after his master, but he did not understand. So, he just stayed with me in distress. I did not have anything to hold on to, so I had to crawl to the gate post which was about 150 yards away. I was finally able to get up, but my ankle shot pain throughout my entire left leg. I walked in excruciating pain to the gate post, and then to the house, which was an additional 50 yards away. I immediately went to the bathtub and cleaned my face and soaked my injury, until Ted came in and asked me what happened. By that time, my ankle was swollen and purple in color. Ted reassured me that I would be fine, and we both said a prayer in faith. He helped me to the bed, where I was able to write this letter to you. *Always, Lorelei.*"

Donna Marie did not think much about the letter until about a week later, when Lorelei called her on the phone. It was the first thing Donna Marie asked her: "Lorelei, are you okay? I received your letter about your injury." Lorelei replied in a cryptic tone: "Oh, it is not much better. I went to have it x-rayed, and the results were inconclusive, so I don't really want to talk about it. Please do not tell anyone else, okay?" So, they talked about other trivial things, but Donna Marie felt uneasy about her sister brushing off her condition. She also wondered why she had called, if she had not wanted to talk more about her injury.

Donna Marie found out later that Lorelei had called a Church practitioner to help her heal the injury. Lorelei had also been a part-time practitioner herself years ago. She once officiated a Church funeral for a retired practitioner. She knew the ramifications of injuries and felt she had the strength and knowledge to overcome it. Ted devotedly read to her every evening from The Bible and from the Science and Health by Mary Baker Eddy. One excerpt from the Science and Health, he continually read to her in his tenderest voice: "Jesus' spiritual origin and understanding enabled him to demonstrate the facts of being, to prove irrefutably how spiritual Truth destroys material error, heals sickness, and overcomes death." (page 315) The correlated verse from the Bible was, "Be good to your servant and I shall live, I shall observe your word. Open my eyes: I shall concentrate on the marvels of your Law." (Psalms 119: 17-19)

As there was never a formal doctor inquiry, only the x-ray, Lorelei and Ted presumed it was either some type of cancer or a blood clot. One of the nurses from the x-ray center called one day to encourage Lorelei to follow up with a doctor she recommended, but Lorelei refused. She and Ted had talked about going to the doctor or the emergency room, but they both felt they could heal it themselves.

Although she was not able to continue with her farm chores, she continued writing, reading and researching from her bed and was working on her next novel. She was writing about the musical and theatrical talents of Walter Stone. He was a screenwriter and producer from the Boston area in the early 1900's. So, writing and research was a solace for her suffering days.

During one of her most painful days, Ted brought in her favorite farm animal, the Cheviot, Hercules. He put Hercules in her lap, and she petted and cooed at him. For a moment, Ted could see in Lorelei's eyes, as she looked up at him, the love that had been missing in their marriage, the tender love that two lovers should have shared all those years. He spoke to her candidly, as never before: "Lorei, you are a woman of such high education, graceful beauty and amazing talents! Yes, I needed a wife to help me on the farm, but why was I so selfish to expect you to sacrifice your life for mine? Why did I think you could love me, as I love you? Why did you marry me? Was it my pleading eyes?" Lorelei still held the precious Hercules in her arms, as she looked at Ted in her tenderest moment ever: "Do you want to really know why I married you, honey? Do you really want to know if I think you lured me to the altar? Honey, I found out many years ago that it did not take a Ph.D. to know where I belonged. Yes, there were also a few obstacles in my drama career, where I knew I needed to move on, but I also knew that it would not be the essence of my life. Ted, you are my essence. Your dedication and hard work to your profession as a farmer, and your honesty and steadfast Christian faith lured me to marry you. Lured is a good word, not bad. I wouldn't change my decision for the world!" Ted's tears blurred, as he knelt down by her bedside and gave her a tender, loving kiss, almost crushing Hercules between them. He took Hercules from her and told her she needed to rest. She blew him another kiss, as he went out of the room.

Ted felt as if he was re-living the horrifying months with his first wife, Cleo, as she suffered from breast cancer. She also was a Christian and faithful wife, who refused to believe that she was really dying. In denial, she had given up hope. He prayed that Lorelei would not do the same.

Chapter Thirteen:

The Consequence

During Lorelei's convalescence, in the ninth month, she had the world news on the radio, as she often did, when she was not writing or sleeping. It had not been a good day. She had been in constant pain throughout her leg and ankle. On her radio that had a little static, she suddenly heard alarming news: "Renowned Art Collector, Humberto Z— just passed away today at the age of 62, in his Pascal shop at the Amalfi Coast. He had a sudden heart attack. His brother was with him and rushed him to the hospital, but he died on the way." Lorelei sat there in shock: "It has to be my Humberto, even though I did not hear clearly the last name! I have forced my heart not to think of him since seeing him in New York. Now, he is dead!" Lorelei took a deep breath, said a lengthy prayer for him and sighed: "What truly happened that secret evening in Italy:"

Lorelei and Humberto left the Italian restaurant about nine. As they walked out of the restaurant arm-in-arm, he asked if she would like to walk on the secluded beach below. She nodded, yes. The weather was perfect, the stars were shining, and Lorelei was in a fairytale. She looked dreamingly into Humberto's eyes. After about a mile of walking, Humberto noticed a shelter of large rocks, like a cave, about a quarter mile hidden from the shore. He asked Lorelei if she would like to sit down a moment and rest. She nodded, yes. And then it happened. He sweetly and gently began kissing her, first from her forehead, to her eyes, to her nose, to her mouth, to her neck, to her breasts and to her toes, which were quivering in emotion. It was like a black-and-white, slow-motion movie, in which each movement of his lips lured Lorelei to respond in euphoria. She was only in the moment, because she knew she would never have that moment again. She was "The Lorelei," who had climbed down from her place on *Her Rock* and had followed her lover in spirit. As they both had been standing and leaning on the rocks, Humberto leaned in to bring down her beautiful, blue gown. She in turn helped him remove his smoky, gray suit and tie. In the moonlit, starry sky, they looked at each other and smiled. Humberto whispered to her: "Siete Mozzafiato!" She blushed and complimented him: "Siete Magnifici!" Humberto carefully laid out their clothes and her pink shawl to put underneath them. Their lips met, Lorelei swooned, and he caught her in his arms. She was a future character in one of her novels and nothing else mattered in the entire world. He held her gently down, as their inner bodies melted in communication with their inner souls.

Lorelei felt another pain in her leg, but she continued her thoughts. When the passion was exhausted, she knew she had to tell him about Ted and their engagement. He listened while holding her in his arms. He knew without further explanation, that she had made her choice, but he wanted to tell her how he felt: "Lorelei, you have just given me a night to remember for the rest of my life, and although I do not agree with your decision to leave me and to accept your fate in Iowa, I want you to know that if you ever need me again, I will come to you. All you have to do is call me. I love you, forever." Lorelei wept softly in his arms, as the sound of the waves echoed in the distance. At almost midnight, they dressed and walked back up to his car, got inside and drove back to the hotel. Lorelei and Humberto walked into the lobby of the hotel and saw David, sleeping and waiting, for his aunt. Humberto kissed her forehead and whispered: "Take care of your nephew, who loves you very much." He said goodnight to her, and that is when she sat across from David, smiling and waiting for him to wake up.

Lorelei's life was a flashback. She had accomplished her aspirations for writing, teaching and travelling, and yet, something had been missing in her life, ever since Fred sat across from her in '64 and told her he found another woman. So, what was happiness? Did one have to have daily romance and love to be happy? What about Ted? Was she not happy living on a farm, producing cotton and hay for her fellow Americans? Didn't she feel loved and needed? Yes, maybe needed, but she was not sure about the love. Ted was neither passionate nor romantic. He was like a robotic farmer, who routinely managed to do his chores and thanked his wife when he knew she was depressed. He appreciated Lorelei, but did he truly love her as he had loved his first wife? Why did Lorelei deny Humberto's eternal love? Was he not the representation of the European life she could have pursued? Why had she not chosen him that evening in Italy? Could she have grown to love Claude, even though he was a cousin? Why did she choose Ted? Why was her life threatened to be taken away because of that choice? She had so many questions that were unanswered.

She knew she would always be faithful to Ted from the moment she had said her wedding vows. She had moments when she spoke to herself: "What if I had chosen Humberto instead of Ted? Would I have been happier in Italy? Would Humberto really have been faithful to me, as he was so handsome and could get any woman he wanted? Why did he want me? She knew his love was genuine! She knew he would have married her if she had stayed. She also felt responsible for his heart attack. Could she have prevented his heart attack?" She wondered if he had finally died from a broken heart, perhaps waiting to see her again?

She suddenly felt a burning ache in her heart and an enpasse of her convictions from her flashback. Perhaps, she did give up hope, or perhaps she was just so tired of living.

Two days later, ten years after her own father's death, and 16 years of marriage to Ted, Lorelei passed away. Ted found her hands in front of her chest in the form of prayer, perhaps asking for forgiveness. She went to her grave carrying her soulful, secret heart, that she never had the chance to even tell her closest sister. She would not ever know that Ted was the only one that really knew.

At Lorelei's funeral, it felt surreal, as everyone could see and hear the rain pouring down outside the church windows. As Donna Marie sat in the front pew by her sister, Marty, she whispered a quote from an old Victorian superstition: "Rain is a heavenly symbol." Marty reached out to hold her sister's hand and nodded in agreement. The organist played the calming hymn, "O Gentle Presence" by Mary Baker Eddy.

Ted knew he would find the right time to read the Will and to decide what plans he would make for his and Lorelei's meager savings. He was very disheartened, as he had been with the early demise of his first wife.

Donna Marie made the trip personally to Indiana, before attending the funeral of her sister. She had to tell their mother. When the nurse made the announcement to Mary that she had a visitor, she could tell right away, when Donna Marie walked in that something horrible had happened. Donna Marie ran into her mother's arms and wept: "Mother, Lorelei has passed away. What am I going to do without her?" She sat on her mother's lap, and she held her in her arms, as if it was just the other day that she use to rock her. It had not mattered how much time had passed between them or of years wasted. What mattered was that her mother was there for her that day, as she needed her more than ever. Mary did not have any answers, but Donna Marie left with some comfort to guide her for the funeral service the next day.

Everyone was somber in their appearances and wore the traditional black suits and dresses. They were all saddened by the news of her painful journey. Steve put his arm around his brother, David's shoulder as he heard him say, "I cannot believe our aunt is gone so early in her life. She was so happy in Europe and wanted us to have a wonderful time, which we did. I will never forget her!" Steve responded to his brother, "You knew her better than Viki or me, and you will be able to keep her memory alive by sharing her adventures to your children and grandchildren." Viki overheard and added, "I will write a novel someday about her life, adventures, dreams and achievements! She must never be forgotten!" As Viki spoke those promising words, Patricia softly added: "Yes, Lorelei will not be forgotten. Her heart-warming letters over the years that your mother has shared with everyone, definitely tells her story. She was a true blessing to her family, husband and literary world."

From Germany, Claude and Hanna had also arrived for the funeral. He spoke, his voice quavering to Hanna: "Lorelei's life has been taken prematurely, a woman of such vibrancy and love. It is so sad." Hanna hugged her father and in agreement said, "Dad, just the one time I met her, I knew she was so special. She was so full of life and love for everyone she met! We will all miss her."

Hanna reminisced with David and shared photos of her exchange student visit with his mother, Donna Marie, Steve and Viki. She had a photo album she entitled, "Hanna's Little Adventure." She had memorable photos of the Civil War Cyclorama, Stone Mountain, Kennesaw Mountain, Six Flags and Calloway Gardens. She was so very grateful and said she had some exciting news. She looked over at David. Her voice was modulated, because she wanted him to know that she had cared deeply for him: "I am engaged to a German friend back home, whom I met after coming home from my visit in the U.S. He also had

been a student with a host family in
Arizona. He was able to see the Grand
Canyon, Tombstone, Sedona and the
Petrified Forest! We are to be married in
December and will spend our honeymoon
in Italy!" Everyone congratulated Hanna,
and David gave her a special cousin's hug
with a little humor: "Cuz, visit soon after
you are married, and we will take your new
husband on the scream machine at Six Flags
and to see our famous gorilla, Willie B., at
the Zoo! We will initiate him into your
Southern family!" Hanna's laugh was
infectious, as everyone agreed with David's
invitation.

Lara and Stewart were in attendance as a
happily, married couple to pay their
respects to their beloved friend. She even
brought the special '69 album she had
organized in Europe to share with everyone
in honor of Lorelei. They approached their
comrade, David, with a group hug. Stewart
and Lara together chimed: "If it had not
been for Lorelei, we would not have had the

opportunity to have fallen in love." David wholeheartedly agreed and they talked about some of their experiences of ten years ago. Eileen came up by David's side, and David introduced his wife to them. Eileen's southern accent was even thicker than David's: "Ya'll, I feel like I already know you, because of your correspondence through the years!"

Lorelei's other siblings were also at her funeral, including Marty and Donald and her half sister, Elaine. Elaine was her younger sister from her father's 2nd marriage, lived in Tennessee and had a successful herb garden. Her mother had been one-half Cherokee Indian, so Elaine had similar features. She also had an estranged, younger brother, Freddie. She spoke fondly of her sister: "Even though Lorelei and I were not that close, as she was with Donna Marie, Lorelei was a model of ambition, of someone who had a goal to be a writer, and she achieved that goal." Marty took Elaine's hand and responded with: "Donald and I were at her wedding sixteen years ago, and I told him at that time that I was not sure she was really cut out for a farmer's type of life. I feel so bad that I may have been right." Donald held up his hand in a fist and replied to Marty: "Yes, the fertilizers, insecticides and manure killed her! She was meant to be a best-seller or an actress on the stage, not a farmer's wife! I am thoroughly disgusted that Ted did not care nor understand that Lorelei was not suitable for farm life!" Ted happened to walk by, as Donald said those cruel words. He defended himself in a rough voice: "Lorelei knew what she was doing when she chose to marry me. She was an avid learner for life, whether it had been as a farmer, a professor or writer. She was aware of the dangers of farm life. Please leave her at peace." Donald walked away, and Marty followed. Only Elaine stayed behind to console Ted, as she saw that his roughness had turned into guilt, as he cried out: "I loved her! I truly did! She was my world, and she helped me continue a tradition of farming that my father had started so many years ago. I wish it had been me, who died instead of her." Elaine gave him a warm hug.

Everyone at Lorelei's funeral also discussed the *Space Shuttle Challenger* tragedy, earlier that year that had exploded upon launching at Cape Canaveral, Florida, killing all seven astronauts. The "Teacher in Space" project had chosen Christa McAuliffe, a high school teacher from Concord, and she would have been the first teacher in space. It was a similar misfortune of a teacher's demise.

Otto and Celia arrived at the memorial service. Otto was in his 80s and Celia took care of him. Celia would have no descendant for her father's farm, which had been a gift from their father, Henry, in addition to the 200 acres from Ted's. Celia would be selling the farm to close neighbors they had known for almost a century.

In Lorelei's attic, Viki and Elaine discovered that the pinewood cabinet with the ancestor notebooks and journals had a label marked "For Viki." One of the albums on the very top was the one that her aunt had recently acquired from Jeannie, their distant cousin. Lorelei had known that she could entrust her genealogy efforts to Viki, who would continue the family research. Viki just had to figure out how to ship or mail it back to her home, but she would honor that trust. Elaine found the "Mermaid and Lover" statue that Humberto had given Lorelei in Italy. She went to David, Lara and Stewart and asked them about it: "Who gave Lorelei this beautiful statue?" Lara sincerely replied, "It was a nice Italian man who gave us all a statue from his own collection. I received one also of a young maiden." Donna Marie came up to the attic to check on Viki and Elaine. She did not want anything of her sister's. It was just too sad. However, when Viki discovered the wedding gift that Aunt Hope had given her, the heirloom quilt, Donna Marie knew that Lorelei would have wanted her to keep it in the family, so she said she would put it in her suitcase to take home. There were also a few other wedding gifts that looked like they had never been used, and Elaine found the ancestral photo frame that Claude and Hanna had given Lorelei. It did not even have a picture in it after all these years. Since Viki was going to be the family historian, Elaine gave the frame to her to keep for future generations. Elaine took some of Lorelei's sweaters and scarves after asking Ted for permission. He was so distraught that he just nodded in slow motion.

In the afternoon after the funeral services, Ted handed Lorelei's cherished sister, Donna Marie, an envelope that was addressed confidentially to her. In it was $5,000.00 worth of savings bonds with her name as the beneficiary. Donna Marie, in tears, asked Ted, "Did you know about this? Are you sure she would want me to have these bonds?" Ted earnestly replied, "Yes, I know that Lorelei loved you very much and wanted to help you financially with your childrens' college educations." In a more serious, somber tone, he then said to Donna Marie: "Would you please go ask your son, David, and your daughter-in-law, Eileen, to meet me here in the living room?" Donna Marie nodded and said she would find them.

Ted motioned for David, Eileen and Donna Marie to follow him in to the living room, and then he closed the door. The other funeral attendees wondered what was happening behind those closed doors. Ted took out his and Lorelei's Will from his top drawer and told them his attorney would be there later to officially read it, but he wanted to go ahead and show them the preliminaries. David and Eileen sat together holding hands, not sure what to expect. Donna Marie looked at Ted, as he began to speak to David: "Lorelei and I thought about our decision for over ten years, ever since you and Eileen made that surprise visit in '74. We talked it over with my brother and niece also, and as you may know, we have no descendants of our own.

My farm was bought in 1850 by my father, Henry, and as you also know, your aunt worked with me side-by-side for sixteen years. She sacrificed her life. She could have lived in Italy with an Italian man who I know loved her deeply, more than I could have ever loved her. But she made a commitment to me. I cannot bring her back to life. But I can give her loved ones a chance to inherit a 200-acre farm that will hopefully bring you prosperity and honor to Lorelei. Therefore, we have in our Will that no matter which one of us passed away first, David, you and Eileen, are the chosen heirs. I hope you will accept this offer."

At first, David ignored Ted's revelation about Humberto. Ted had not been blind, after all. He had known all along that Lorelei loved another. However, in respect and promise to his aunt, he did not respond to that revelation. He looked at his wife with his eyelids raised in question. They were both surprised at the offer. They thought perhaps the Will had something in it for

Donna Marie, as her closest sister, and that they were just in there as witnesses. They did not have appropriate words, because they had not been prepared. Eileen motioned for David to say something: "Ted, we appreciate your offer. However, what does it mean for you? Do you want to continue living on the farm?" Ted answered, "I am getting very old. Remember, I was 22 years older than your aunt. It is time that I move into a retirement home. Perhaps your mother would also like to come and live with you on the farm?" Donna Marie looked at her son. She had tears in her eyes, "What a thoughtful gift that my sister and brother-in-law has given you! I would be happy living with you and Eileen and helping you on the farm. Steve is married and settled in his own business, and Viki is away at college, so it would be a good time of transition for us. What do you think?" David and Eileen, looking up to heaven, spoke: "Yes, Ted, we accept your kind offer. Thank you." They started to get up, but then

Ted remembered the map. He took the treasure chest map out of his pocket and handed it to David: "This map is also part of your inheritance. Your creative aunt devised a map to lead you to the treasure chest, somewhere within the 200 acres of this farm, that she wanted you to have. Do you have any questions?" David was serious but comical as his aunt would want him to be: "Even in her death, she has found an unselfish way to make a somber service more festive. We will share this with everyone, so they can help us find the treasure. Thank you."

They came out of the living room's closed doors in a most reverent attitude and shared the news.

Donald was the first to question Ted, as he walked out behind David and Eileen: "Had my sister also considered her own brother and sisters? I am okay, of course, with your choice, because they will make great farmers, but I was just curious if she considered the rest of us?" Ted answered:

"Yes, we considered <u>every</u> <u>one</u> of her family members. We weighed all the options, including education and experience. I will not be giving you the specific reasons for our choice at this time, because I do not feel the time is appropriate, but if you want to ask me in the future, you may." "Oh, I almost forgot," Ted continued. He pulled out of his suit pocket three more envelopes. He gave one to Elaine, Donald and Marty. Standing there in front of everyone, they each opened up their envelopes. Inside each was a thousand dollar check. Lorelei had not forgotten her other siblings afterall.

David and Eileen stepped in to show the treasure map. Everyone was curious enough to help in the search, except Ted bowed out. He did not want anyone knowing that he knew where the treasure was. They hugged David and Eileen and congratulated their new future, and then they all walked outside to begin the search.

The map looked like a pirate's map. Lorelei had drawn landmarks, including the barn and tool shed. She led them around the farm house, through the pasture, past the sheep and past her exotic garden. Before they all realized it, she had given them a tour of the entire 200 acres. Then, Donald helped decipher the coded marks that represented the steps to the final oak tree. However, the spot had not been marked, so several shovels were brought out, and Donald, David and Steve dug holes all around the oak. Finally, after two hours, as providence would have it, David was the one who found the correct hole. He uncovered the chest, lifted it up to Eileen, and she helped her husband up to the surface. Together, they opened the chest, while everyone else gathered around, and inside were the special European coins and silver dollars. Everyone could see that as a total, they were probably worth a good bit of money. On top was a note written only for David and Eileen. As they read the note to themselves first, David had tears in his eyes, and then he read it, looking at his mother: "Dear David and Eileen, this treasure chest is for you and your descendants. These are the special coins that I saved from our European adventure together and my previous tours. I want you to save them for many years, because they will be worth more, especially the American silver dollars. I love you, Godson. Please give your wife and mother a hug for me. *Always, Aunt Lorelei.*" By the time David finished reading the note, all the women were in tears, and the men were shaking their heads thinking of how Lorelei had even brought drama to her own funeral service.

On the final day, when everyone was leaving to drive or fly back to their homes, Viki and Elaine walked by the small flock of sheep. Viki made a fervent observation: "See how the sheep are staring at us, as if they know that their mistress, Lorelei, has passed away. Lorelei's, own Christie-Lee, especially looked as if she had tears in her eyes." Elaine also noticed something peculiar about the sheep: "Look at the Cheviot one over standing by himself. I remember one of

Lorelei's letters saying that she named him, Hercules. He looks as if he is angry with the world." It was an eerie moment for Elaine and Viki, that they would always remember.

A memorial was established in Lorelei's name at Iowa Wesleyan College. Funeral services were held at the Elliott Chapel in New London and interment was in Trinity Cemetery, the same Cemetery where Ted's first wife was buried, and where he would eventually be buried.

Two months later, Donna Marie, David and Eileen moved from Georgia to Iowa to take over Ted and Lorelei's farm. Ted was comfortable at a nursing home nearby, and they would visit him often. David hired several farm-hands and acquired modern tools. Eileen became the preacher at the nearby Church and a devoted farmer's wife. Donna Marie maintained Lorelei's exotic garden and looked healthier than she had in years. By the end of 1986, the "Brannon Family Farm" was doing well, and a new story would be told by the baby-on-the-way.

Author's Bibliographical Notes:

Excerpts abstracted from <u>1,001 Broadways</u> <u>Hometown Talent on Stage</u> by Lorelei F. Eckey, Maxine Allen and William T. Schoyer, The Iowa State University Press, Ames, Iowa, 1982.

Excerpt from the February 1982 article by Lorelei Eckey in *The Palimpsest,* Iowa's Popular History Magazine, "Pilgrims of the Impossible."

Excerpt from the January 1984 article by Lorelei Eckey in *The Christian Science Monitor.*

Excerpt from the February 1984 article by Lorelei Eckey in the Mt. Pleasant's *The News,*

"Home Talent Shows Cut Loose in Mt. Pleasant After War."

Excerpts from several articles in 1977 by Lorelei Eckey in the Mt. Pleasant's *The News*, "Out on the Farm."

Excerpt from the February 1984 article by Lorelei Eckey in the *Missouri Historical Review*, "Home Talent Shows in the 20s Were Snappy."

Historical facts abstracted from *google.com*.

Notes abstracted from journals, letters and postcards.

About the Author:

Vicki Boartfield is the author of her first family novel. She is a former middle and high school English teacher. She is also the family historian and has written several articles for <u>Genealogy Today</u>. Vicki and her husband, Albert, reside in Coolidge, Arizona. They have been members of the United Methodist Church for over 35 years. They have five grown children and are looking forward to grandchildren soon.

CPSIA information can be obtained
at www.ICGtesting.com
Printed in the USA
FFOW04n1029070314
4105FF